I0667756

Runaway
A Story of Hagar

Charles Millson

GRAVE DISTRACTIONS PUBLICATIONS
NASHVILLE, TENNESSEE

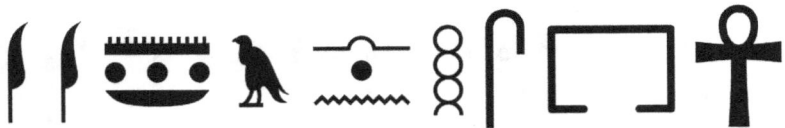

Grave Distractions Publications

Nashville, Tennessee

www.gravedistractions.com

Copyright © 2017 Charles Millson

ISBN-13: 978-1-944066-19-2

In Publication Data

Millson, Charles

Primary BISAC Category: FIC026000

FICTION / Religious

Secondary BISAC Category: FIC046000

FICTION / Jewish

Printed in the United States

READ THIS FIRST

G rowing up in a churched household, I knew the stories of the book of Genesis before I could read. In my youth, the heroes of the Bible and the nation of Israel loomed large in my boyish imagination. Part of my love of history stems from my early education in the Bible stories told me by my mother and my Sunday school teachers.

By college age, I came to understand a little better that *the purpose of the Bible is not now nor was it ever meant to be a history.* That doesn't mean that the Bible isn't truth; I believe it is truth. What I mean is that the stories almost always have meanings that are not meant to be taken as history. And rather than diminish these tales in my heart, this idea challenged me to see the universal application in the stories far above and beyond any idea of "history" as we know it.

Think of it this way: Would you take a history book and try to make it a religious book? To try to do the opposite is just as absurd.

To try to "prove" the Bible as a historically accurate book only serves to diminish its usefulness as a book of truth. For example, George Washington has the reputation of being an honest man. We recite the story of the cherry tree as proof. We even add a quote to it: "I cannot tell a lie." Yet, that tale never happened. Does it matter? No. The point of the story is to show an example of Mr. Washington's honesty. The story accomplishes this, even if the story is not history.

Would we say, "I'll take this travel guide and read it as a cookbook?" True, the travel guide may have recipes in it, and it may even have details of culinary norms and a history of cooking in that land. The author may even have a background in cooking. Again, however, I would miss the purpose of the book as a travel guide.

I say all that in order to point out that Abraham and his story are important far, far beyond the fact that we have no historical proof that such a man ever lived. Remember before when I said that Israel seemed so large to me as a young person? I also meant that Israel, in my mind, was as important a nation as Egypt, Assyria, Babylon, or Persia. Such a notion is, in historical reality, simply untrue. That doesn't mean that Israel isn't significant to us. It is. However, it was never big or politically or militarily powerful.

Israel was, at its greatest, not much more than a collection of tribes and towns centered around the hilly areas of Canaan—and that for a relatively short period of time. And one of the major reasons Israel could never establish itself beyond the area we know is because the two great cradles of civilization that bookended the area—the Nile (Egypt) and Mesopotamia (Assyria, Babylon, Persia, and other empires) to the northwest—were the powerful areas.

The sliver of earth that we know of as Israel/Canaan was the "land bridge" between these two great and rival civilizations. As one or the other civilization grew powerful, it extended its power/ control over this land bridge area. When the two areas declared war on each other (which was often), Canaan was the area where they most frequently met. Control of it (especially the part near the coastal areas and the fertile Jezreel Valley) meant you controlled trade, access, and the front line of protection of your homeland.

So, for much of the history of the Israelites, the people and land were controlled by either Egypt or a Mesopotamian power— whichever one was more powerful at the moment. When Israel had flashes of relative power and peace, it was because of a time of troubles or unrest in these two greater civilized areas. Trouble in Egypt and Mesopotamia meant the peoples of this in-between land could have a greater say in what they wanted to do.

And remember, Israel wasn't the only group in the area. Canaan was occupied by the Canaanites, including such tribes as (depending on the time) Philistines, Phoenicians, Moabites, Amorites, Jebusites, Syrians, and several other peoples. In fact, Israel wasn't even the most powerful group of people in this area by far; it was weak, small, and heavily influenced by the other peoples and nations around it.

All that cultural history makes Abraham the perfect "father" for Israel. In his story, he comes from Mesopotamia, goes to Canaan, travels to Egypt, and back to Canaan. He is a Hebrew but he cannot be separated from his ties to these two civilizational bookends of Canaan. He is nomadic, a shepherd, and a polygamist. His sons and his grandsons and his great grandchildren all were, too, for the most part. One of his sons goes to Egypt to find a wife (Ishmael); another goes to Mesopotamia to marry (Isaac). One of his grandsons also goes to Mesopotamia to marry and dies in Egypt (Jacob). All of the lives of the patriarchs of the Hebrew Bible symbolize that great migration of peoples from the north to the south and back again that was the reality of Canaan two millennia ago.

That is not all. One can easily see the common thread in all this as it continues in the Christian Bible, where we find the Jesus birth stories that have wise men come to him from Mesopotamia (the "East") and have his small family run away from Herod to Egypt for refuge. Invoking both powerful nearby areas, Mesopotamia and Egypt (despite the fact that by the time of Christ, Rome ruled almost all the known world), makes Jesus fit perfectly into the stories about the Patriarchs.

The dates chosen for this Bible-based book you now hold rely on imperfect guesses as to when Abraham lived; again, the Bible is not history and to rely on it for such is foolhardy if this were an academic book. It is Bible-based fiction, luckily, and we can thus use the Bible to guess that Abraham lived roughly 2,000 years before Jesus, 500 or so years before Moses, and about 1,000 years before King David. That "rough" estimate allows for some interesting guessing as to when, exactly, Abraham and Sarah would have traveled to Egypt, for example.

Therefore, I chose to make the date for this book sometime about 2,050 years before the birth of Jesus or, in other words, about 4,000 years ago. That allowed me to describe in this book a divided Egypt, with southern (Upper) Egypt being ruled by one pharaoh and northern (Lower) Egypt being ruled by another. To try to explain this better, a map is provided for you, but it also helps to remember that the Nile flows north, and that makes the northern part of the river "Lower" Egypt. Most of the book doesn't even take place there, but I wanted you to know all that before you read.

We read in Genesis that Ishmael does return to the land of his father to help his brother, Isaac, bury Abraham. I've always wondered if that meeting was awkward or if the brothers let bygones be bygones and embraced each other. Isaac is the one patriarch we concentrate on the least—at least compared to his father and youngest son (Jacob). It is difficult to get a clear picture of him since we have so little information about him from the Genesis narrative.

But this book is about Hagar, and we know painfully even less about her. Yet, her story is one of the most remarkable in the entire Bible.

We don't even know her real name. It surprised me to realize that Hagar wasn't the name she was born with. Hagar means "runaway"; that name is, like many in the Bible, the one assigned to her based on qualities shown in the story. Twice (at least) Hagar runs away or "leaves" or "flees." In Hebrew, the name "Hagar" can mean all these things.

The name "Ramla" is completely my invention. I wanted to choose an Egyptian name that had a meaning that could have fit her personality and what we know of her. Besides, since that name means, "prophetess," I thought it would be appropriate given her unusual and uncanny ability to converse with a God she did not know and did not worship where and as she grew up.

One of the most important things about her is, of course, her relationship with God as described in Genesis. When we meet her in the text, she is described as the Egyptian servant of Sarah, Abraham's wife. Abraham and Sarah had only recently left Egypt when Hagar is introduced. It is not a stretch of the imagination to believe they acquired her there—especially when we read in Genesis that pharaoh gave Abraham gifts including servants. So, it is also not difficult to believe that Hagar grew up a polytheist like everyone else in Egypt.

We do not talk much in church about the (most probably) huge age discrepancy between Abraham and Hagar when she is required to have a child by him. The story says he was in his ninth decade when that happens; he is probably old enough to be her grandfather. While this disturbs our modern sensibilities, such a practice was common in most parts of the world (and, sadly, still common in some parts) until the last few centuries.

Some commentators and theologians argue that Sarah's offer of Hagar to Abraham is "sinful" because she has no faith that God will bring the promise to fruition. However, God never specified that Sarah was to be the one who would bear the child—at least not until his promise to Abraham and Sarah in Genesis 17. Until then, God doesn't say who the mother of all these countless descendants will be. If it was a sin, then why does God allow Hagar to get pregnant? Why does He stop her when she runs away to go back home—why send her back to Abraham if Ishmael is the product of a "sinful" union?

For me, Hagar is the victim here; she had no choice in any of this. However, being the product of 21st century mentality, I have given her a choice in this story.

And the idea that the God of Abraham would speak to her in the desert is incredibly…well, it's pretty incredible.

And when God speaks to her she shows no surprise, and she doesn't lie to Him. She has been with Abraham as Sarah's servant for about a decade at that point—if we are to assume Sarah received her when she and Abraham were in Egypt. But for someone who is not supposed to know about such happenings, Hagar seems relatively calm about having a conversation with Abraham's God. However, she then gives God a nickname or a "pet name"—she calls Him "God-Who-Sees-Me"—and then the text suggests that the two of them maintained a running conversation from that point on. That's not something God seems to have done with Sarah even though we might expect that He would have.

The story of Sodom (the neighboring town of Gomorrah gets thrown in with Sodom in the destruction if not the actual story leading up to it) has been twisted and used by so many people throughout history to prove many things that the story didn't necessarily intend to teach. The easy way to identify the reason God destroys Sodom is to say that God hates homosexuality. That's not what the Hebrew text says, however, neither there nor elsewhere. If you read it closely, you'll see that the men in Sodom were, at best, bisexual—and, even at that, there's something deeper and more important going on there other than sexual issues.[1]

Look at Ezekiel 16, beginning in verse 48. The sins of Sodom, the text says, include "Pride, excess of food, and prosperous ease, but (they) did not aid the poor and needy." In other words, the sin of Sodom is really greed—the selfish accumulation of stuff—and the inability to share what you have with those who have not. Sounds too close to home, doesn't it? Ezekiel goes on to say that Israel's sins were worse than Sodom's, but you won't hear any of that preached anywhere anytime soon. In the story that you have in front of you, I have Hagar call their sin "ingratitude," and that's really at the root of what is happening in Sodom. Selfishness, "what's in this for me,"

---

[1]Same-sex relationships (mostly male) were not uncommon in the ancient near east; such are found in the literature and art of both Mesopotamia and Egypt.

and pride are sins of ingratitude that affect each of us today much as they did in Sodom and only *sometimes* have expression in all types of sexual conduct, both straight and gay.

I have also tried to follow the outline of the Genesis narrative in telling this story. Genesis 12 is Egypt. Chapter 13 through 14:16 takes us back to Bethel and tells of Lot's issues with the kings of the river valley. Chapters 14:17-15, 21 tells of Melchizedek and the covenant ceremony. Genesis 16 is where we first "meet" Hagar in the text. Chapter 17 takes us up to the promise God makes to Sarah. (By the way, circumcision, which is introduced to Abraham and all the males in his group in chapter 17, was never practiced by Mesopotamian civilizations. It is an Egyptian custom. Who better to introduce it to Abraham than Hagar herself?) Chapters 18 and 19 describe the visitors from the Lord and the story of Sodom and Lot's family. Chapters 20 through 21:7 contain the story of Isaac's birth and Abimelech. Chapter 21:8-14 tells of the "weaning party" and Abraham sending Hagar and Ishmael out of the camp. We last see/hear from Hagar in chapter 21:15-21. Then, in a conclusion (the story of which actually begins this book), we are told in Genesis Chapter 25 that Ishmael and Isaac bury their father together. If you read the Bible story along with the chapters as you go, you will see where I have had to make fictionalized dialogue and events and even people to fill in the gaps where the Bible narrative is achingly and frustratingly vague or short. Again, read the Genesis narrative. There's so much we miss even if details are scant in places.

You will read the name "El" for God in this book. El is a simple name for God that means, well, "God." You see that name in many of the proper names of the Bible: Bethel (House of God), Israel (Wrestles with God), Samuel, etc. God does call Himself "God

Almighty" before Abraham, a name that comes to us as *El Shaddai*. To avoid confusion, I did not use this name in the book. God for the most part is simply called "El" here.

Men and women look at the Bible differently. Do such differences matter? Yes. Do they shape the way each gender sees God? Yes, again. Can a man write a book about the experience of a woman in the Bible? Should he? These last two questions remain unanswered. I will fully admit that a woman would be better suited to do so.

In the writing of this book, I hope to show the reader that, like Hagar, we, too, find ourselves in spiritual deserts during our lifetimes. We also seek our own ways—we become runaways— and we often leave situations where God has put us. But, for the spiritually aware, the God-Who-Sees-Me will come to us in our deserts and remind us that He has a plan and we need to trust Him—if we humble ourselves before Him, as Hagar does. He puts us where He wants us. And He has promises of wonderful things in store for us.

In this way, all of us who seek His face are Hagar. It's why her story is so important for believers today.

MAP OF ABRAM'S JOURNEYS

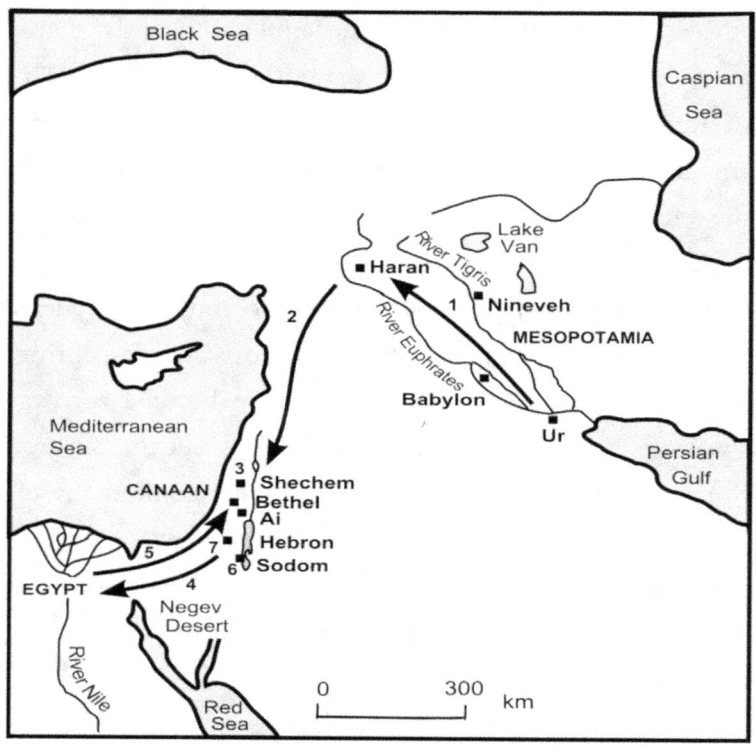

1. Abram born in Ur and moves to Haran with his father and his nephew, Lot.
2. On the way to Canaan, Abram hires Eliezer of Damascus to run his affairs.
3. First altar to El built at Shechem.
4. Travel to Egypt because of famine.
5. Returns to Canaan from Egypt; Hagar acquired possibly.
6. Lot chooses to live near the river, settles at Sodom.
7. Possible final settlement near Hebron.

CHARACTERS AND PLACES

Nomads

Abram/Abraham—From Ur. Husband of Sarai/Sarah and Ramla/ Hagar. Father of Ishmael and Isaac. Abram means "Great or Exalted Father," while Abraham means "Father of Many."

Bracha—Mute servant girl of Ramla/Hagar given to her after her marriage to Abram. Fictional character.

El—God of Abram/Abraham.

Eliezer—A man from Damascus. Hired by Abram to run his business affairs.

Isaac—Son of Sarah and Abraham. Born when Sarah is 90 and Abraham is 100.

Ishmael—Son of Ramla/Hagar and Abram/Abraham. Born when Abram is about 86.

Lot—Abram/Abraham's nephew, the son of his brother. He settles for a time in Sodom.

Ramla/Hagar—Egyptian by birth, servant woman of Sarai. Mother of Ishmael and wife of Abram. Ramla means "Prophetess" while Hagar means "Runaway or Flee." NOTE: The name Ramla is invented for the purposes of this story.

Sarai/Sarah—Wife/Sister of Abram/Abraham. Both names mean "Princess or Noblewoman."

Egyptians

Amunet—The Goddess to whom Ramla/Hagar is dedicated.

Merikare—Ruler of Lower (Northern) Egypt in the 21st century before the Common Era. Marries Sarai. NOTE: Genesis doesn't list the name of the pharaoh who marries Sarai. However, Merikare was an actual pharaoh of Lower Egypt.

Tefibi—Merikare's chief buyer of slaves. He develops a care/concern for Ramla/Hagar. Fictional Character.

Tjetjy—Ramla/Hagar's grandfather. The chamberlain of the pharaoh of Upper Egypt. Fictional Character.

PLACES

Bethel—The name means "House of God". Abram builds an altar here and lives here for a time.

Egypt—During the time of this story, there are two Egypts—Upper (Southern) and Lower (Northern) Egypt. Ramla/Hagar is from Upper Egypt but becomes a slave of the pharaoh of Lower Egypt. It is to Lower Egypt that Abram and Sarai come.

Haran—Abram moves here with his family. It is here that El first speaks to him.

Nen—Nesu—Capital of Lower (Northern) Egypt.

Oaks of Mamre—Abram & Sarai and their servants and flocks live here for a decade or so after Lot takes the "good land" near the river.

Paran—Traditionally, it is the wilderness area that lines the western side of the Arabian Peninsula. Where Ramla/Hagar and Ishmael settle after they leave Abram/Abraham. It is here that Isaac's servants find Ishmael after Abram/Abraham dies.

Shashotep—Merchant town on the border between Upper and Lower Egypt. Ramla/Hagar is sold as a slave here.

Sodom—City on the sea near where the Jordan River empties into it. Lot moves here with his family after he and Abram part ways. Sodom is destroyed by El for its sins.

Ur—Mesopotamian birthplace of Abram/Abraham, Sarai/Sarah, and Lot.

Waset—Capital of Upper (Southern) Egypt. In this story, Ramla/Hagar is born here.

PRELUDE

The young boy ran into the tent. Breathlessly, he managed to say, "f-f-father!" He swallowed hard and continued. "Two riders...from the northwest...coming..." he managed to say as he waved his hands towards his face.

"Slow down, son," the old man said as he sat on large cushions with his supper plate on the tent floor. He calmly reached for his wine cup as the boy worked to gather his breath. "If there are only two of them, then they are either travelers or messengers," the old man said between sips of wine. "Either way, shouldn't we make them welcome?" he asked with a smile.

The boy nodded and grinned. His breathing regulated, and he collected himself. "Now, tell me again," he said to the boy.

"I was going to get the water for donkeys," the boy said, "and I saw the shimmer of movement on the horizon to the northwest." He paused and waited for the old man's approval to continue.

"Good! Then what?"

"I shielded my eyes like you taught me, and saw that there were two riders coming this way. Then I ran to tell you."

The old man was silent for a moment, seeming intent on his meal. "And what of our donkeys?" he said, stirring the gravy in the plate with the flat bread without looking up.

The boy gulped. "I...I left them. I will go get them the water now."

"Wait," the old man said, holding up his free hand. "There is time for the water later. First, go out and take care of our guests. Greet them warmly, Kedemah, when they arrive; give them water, then show them into the tent. And be sure to take care of their animals, my son." The old man then looked up and added with a smile, "and ours."

"Greetings in the name of El. Are you Ishmael, the son of Abraham?" the older-looking of the two men asked when at last the boy brought the strangers inside the tent.

A frown wrinkled the old man's brow. "May El bless you. Yes, my name is Ishmael, but my father's name used to be Abram."

The two messengers looked at each other and nodded in agreement. "Yes," the younger one agreed, "Abram."

The older one continued. "I am Bethuel and this is my brother, Nahor. We bring you word that your father is dead, sir."

Their words seemed to barely register in Ishmael's face. He reached out to the plate and grabbed a hunk of goat meat and brought it to his lips. He smacked the savory meat and licked his brown, wrinkled fingers clean. The long pause as he ate caused the visitors to shift uncomfortably as they stood before him. Perhaps the news did not register in the older man's mind, they thought.

He reached for his drink before he spoke.

"Are you the sons of Bethuel, the son of Millcah? I once knew of one such."

The two men looked at each other with confusion. The younger one spoke. "Yes...we are...but did you understand that we bring news that your father is dead?"

"You must forgive me if I have no reaction to this information," Ishmael said, looking down as he swirled the liquid in his wine cup. "I have had no contact with my father for over 70 years; why would it matter now to me if he were dead or alive? But won't you join me for supper?" he asked, looking up at them.

The messengers again glanced at each other, but this time they searched the other as if each did not know how to react to this. "We have our instructions from your brother and our relative, Isaac," the older of the two men said.

"Isaac?" Ishmael repeated. "My brother? He sent you?" Ishmael asked, his eyes narrowing in suspicion as he for the first time really looked closely at the messengers' faces. "For what purpose?"

Finally, the older messenger felt he was on firmer ground. "Your brother desires that you come to Hebron, the land of your birth, and help him bury your father."

Ishmael's voice rose and his eyes grew wide, his gray, bushy eyebrows arching towards his brow. "My brother...my younger brother...desires? Who is he to desire anything of me?" the old man demanded loudly. "And I know what is my land and what is not!" he added with emphasis. A servant stuck his head inside the tent to see what caused Ishmael to speak like this. Ishmael waved him away with the back of his hand, and the young man ducked his head back outside.

The younger visitor cleared his throat and tried to calm Ishmael. "My brother misspoke," he said, putting his hands up in supplication. "Actually, your brother humbly requests, with great respect, that you honor him by coming to Hebron as his guest and helping him bury your father."

"And look!" the older one said, placing a wooden cask of jewelry and fine items down on the tent floor, "Your brother has sent you these gifts as well!"

"Ah!" Ishmael said smiling broadly, looking with laughing eyes over the little chest and its valuables. He wiped his mouth and beard with the back of his hand and stiffly rose to his feet. "If my little brother 'humbly requests,' then who am I to refuse?" And with that, he held out his arms in a sign of welcome to the two visitors.

‡ ‡ ‡

As Ishmael and his group approached the large collection of tents, he saw, among the throng of people milling around outside of them, a tall gray-bearded man with a long, pointed nose. It had to be Isaac, he thought. The man looked too much like his memories of the father he had not seen in such a long time.

When Ishmael and his company came closer, the milling crowd stopped moving and grew hushed. They parted as waves before him as Ishmael was helped down from his animal, and they allowed a path directly to the tall bearded man.

Ishmael saw that the old man was crying. He hadn't expected this. He thought he might possibly meet suspicion, or hatred, or treachery, or resentment. Tears, he did not foresee.

The man started moving towards him with his arms outstretched. Overcome by his own emotion, Ishmael was surprised to find his own cheeks wet with tears as well. The two old men met in the middle and embraced. The group shouted appreciation for the gesture.

"My brother!" Isaac said into Ishmael's ear, closing his eyes in the hug.

""Yes," Ishmael answered. "My brother," he repeated, resting his head on his taller brother's shoulder.

The crowd murmured appreciatively. Some younger men started moving towards the pair, joining them in the embrace. Soon it was as if the entire crowd, both men and women, were crying and hugging in a circle around the two brothers.

Finally, Isaac pulled away and wiped his face with his hands. "Who is this you have brought?" he said, pointing over the heads of the crowd to the small group behind Ishmael.

"Ah! These are my children!" Ishmael said, his face brightening through his tears. He introduced his two older sons and the three grandchildren who had accompanied him. "There are ten more back at home," Ishmael explained, "but they had to stay to look after the animals."

Isaac bowed slightly in respectful deference to the sons and grandsons as Ishmael introduced each of them. "You say you have more children besides these? Twelve sons?" Isaac asked. "Praise be to El! For He has blessed you, then."

"And He you," Ishmael said, motioning with his arm to the assembled crowd.

Isaac smiled broadly, revealing that even in his old age he had kept most of his teeth. "Yes and no, brother. These children are not all mine. Some of these are cousins and relatives from other families. But," and he paused, searching the group behind him, "these, here," he said, motioning for two of the young men to come forward, "these two are my twins!"

A muscular, heavyset and hairy young man strode through the edge of the group and stiffly bowed low before Ishmael. "This is my oldest, Esau," Isaac explained.

"A fine man!" Ishmael exclaimed as Esau rose and smiled at his uncle. Indeed, the young man's muscles shone through the thick layer of hair on his arms and about his neck. Clearly, this son of Isaac's was not one to cross, Ishmael thought.

"Jacob," Isaac said, motioning for the other one to come forward, "he is my youngest." A slight, almost delicate young man came and bent gracefully at Ishmael's feet and rose.

"Twins?!" Ishmael repeated, his eyes smiling at the differences between the two young men. "May El's blessings be on your sons," Ishmael said to his brother. He placed a hand on each of the boys' heads. "May you each know and find El as your father and grandfather have known and found him."

As the boys stood, Ishmael looked questioningly at the rest of the group. Isaac saw his brother's puzzled look and explained. "Our father—he has other sons?"

Ishmael furrowed his brow in thought, but Isaac scanned the heads of the crowd and continued. "After my mother died, our father took another wife—there she is, Keturah." Isaac pointed in the crowd to a small, middle-aged woman with eyes that sat widely on her head but who seemed unremarkable to Ishmael otherwise. He bent his head slightly towards the woman who returned his bow with one of her own. Isaac continued. "By her, he had sons and even had children by other women as well. So," said Isaac, smiling at Ishmael, "you have other brothers besides me.

Ishmael said nothing for a moment, and he bit his lip in thought. Finally, nodding, he said, "This is good. They can help us bury our father."

‡ ‡ ‡

The cool of the cave at Machpelah was in sharp contrast to the shimmering heat outside. Abraham's body, wrapped in white linen and filled with spices, was stiff but not heavy at all. The old man had lived to be over 170 years old, but Isaac reported that when he died he was still sinewy with musculature. It seemed he was active up until the end.

When the sons of Abraham carried their father into the cave, they spoke very little. Isaac nodded to the place that had been prepared in the cave for her to receive Abraham's body. Kneeling in unison, the sons gently laid the old man's remains in the shallow depression. As was the custom, each son placed a stone around their dead father's body. It was Isaac who said, after the last stone was placed, "He was a prince of El."

When they were finished with the ritual and standing around the pile of stones, Ishmael noticed that Isaac had moved to the back of the cave by himself and now stood looking over another mound of stones. He realized that this other body must be that of Isaac's mother, Sarah. Wanting to allow his brother some time alone, Ishmael motioned for the other sons to go outside, and they all moved out into the warm daylight. Isaac joined them after a few minutes alone inside the cave. He ordered some of his servants to secure the entrance with large stones.

"Let us go back to the tents," Isaac announced. "We will offer sacrifice to El to thank Him for our father. Then, let us sit, eat, drink, and speak of our father." The group murmured agreement.

As they made their way back to the tents, Isaac and Ishmael walked at the rear of the mourners. "Thank you, my brother," Isaac said to Ishmael, grabbing his older brother affectionately by the arm.

Ishmael turned to Isaac in surprise. "Thank me? For what?"

"For coming."

Ishmael turned back towards the group, leaned on his stick, and nodded. The event stirred emotions in Ishmael he didn't know he carried. Touching Isaac's shoulder in affectionate response, he said, "Thank you for asking."

‡   ‡   ‡

That evening, the fire burned lower, but its flames still licked skyward towards the star-filled heavens. By this time, most made their ways to their beds after the feast.

Ishmael and Isaac remained reclined out in the open air on cushions that lay on an expensive carpet at the opening of the tent, each one with a cup of wine before him. Servants in the tent behind them moved around almost wordlessly, picking up the remains of the feast. Talk between a few other relatives who had only just met each other punctuated the night as pleasantries such as, "May you rest well," and "See you in the morning," could be heard in front of tents around them as the camp settled down for the night.

That left the brothers alone for the moment. Both old men, their stomachs full and their hearts heavy, stared out at the fire and the stars and beyond and talked of the father they lost.

"You know that I have no clear memory of you," Isaac said after a moment of silence, propping himself up on one elbow and turning to face Ishmael. "Most of what I remember I cannot separate from what I have dreamed about you in the past years."

"You dream…of me?"

"Yes…of course I do. For years I have done so. Perhaps I remember more the idea of having an older brother that I missed rather than having you in my heart as a true memory," Isaac explained.

"I understand. I was much the same in a way," Ishmael nodded, looking at the fire intently. He chose his words haltingly. "We…we never completely understood why…why our father made us leave."

"We?" Isaac repeated. Then, he understood. "Ah, you and your mother. Of you and your mother we never spoke," Isaac said, tossing back the last of the wine in his cup. "And I never asked." He reached for the ewer and filled his cup again.

"Hagar," Isaac said, and he left the name hanging in the air, and his voice trailed off as if the name itself was the fabric of legend "What I know I learned from my father's…our father's…servants in bits and pieces. And you know how unreliable servants' tales can be." Isaac chuckled softly.

Ishmael's face, by contrast, remained serious, and followed a shooting star as it fell to earth on the horizon. "Her name was Ramla," he said after a moment, gently correcting Isaac. "Hagar is only what your mother called her." He stopped himself there, because he had promised himself on the journey that he would try to avoid uncomfortable talk.

"Yes, of course, 'Runaway'…" Isaac said, nodding and suddenly understanding. Isaac, too, wanted to avoid any controversial subjects.

The brothers remained quiet for some time, looking at the countless stars above them. Isaac took the silent moment to point up and say, "Your descendants will be more numerous than the stars in the sky." He took his eyes off the stars and looked at his brother to see if he understood the reference.

Ishmael nodded and said, "Yes, that's what I've been told El has promised. To our father. To both of us. Sons of the promise we are." Yet, he continued to look upward. He started to speak, but he wanted to make sure that he did not insult this brother that he had found after so many years.

Isaac tried to come to his rescue. "You were going to say something?"

"No," Ishmael said. He quickly corrected himself. "Yes."

"You say your family never spoke of us. That was not true for us. Of you and your mother, Sarai, and our father, we always spoke," he said quietly. His eyes began to moisten, and he lowered them from the whiteness of the stars above to the fire's yellow flames below.

"Here, brother, here," Isaac said, holding the wine ewer, "fill your cup and tell me the story. Please."

Ishmael, turned on his side and faced his brother, propping his head with one bent arm. Isaac could see him thinking as he poured the wine into Ishmael's cup.

"Please?" Isaac repeated.

"Yes," Ishmael said, finally, drying his glistening eyes with the back of an old, weathered hand. "Why not?"

And with that, Ishmael sat up, stiffly crossed his aging legs, and took a long drink of his wine before the fire.

When he had drained it, he set the cup beside him on the carpet and said, "My mother, Ramla, was born in Egypt..."

PART I

RAMLA

ONE

Ramla first remembered the color brown. Her earliest complete memories were of running through the tall, tan reeds next to the riverbank. She remembered looking at her brown legs and sun-kissed bare feet and simple, white cotton child's dress contrasting with the lighter browns and dark brown-green of the rushes and the rust colors of the Great River's mud.

Sometimes her early memories were of a game where her mother would chase her and swoop upon her and snatch her up and kiss her on her neck. "Where are you, my little runaway?" her mother would call as Ramla hid among the reeds. The thrill of being found then chased and the ticklishness of her neck being kissed when she was finally caught made the game Ramla's favorite. There was something inexpressively wonderful about the running and the hiding and the chase and the comfort of knowing she was loved.

Beha, one of the king's dogs, usually accompanied them because Ramla loved him so, and being in the king's household meant that

Beha was theirs, too, after a fashion. Beha, her brown fur billowing in the breeze, would prance and run and nuzzle both mother and daughter as they all three played their game of chase.

Then, after the game, Ramla had flashes of images that her mother would sit with her next to the river and speak of more serious things, some things that Ramla didn't understand at the time and some things she never understood completely.

With age, Ramla realized that life must have been difficult for her mother, being a daughter of Tjetjy, the chief treasurer and king's chamberlain, the sister of yet another palace official, and the wife of one of the king's generals. Palace intrigue was rife in her sheltered world, and from an early age Ramla realized her place was only as an extension of the Great Lord of the Two Lands, Intef, in the City of the Scepter, Waset.

In later years, it pained Ramla that, for all her memories of her time in Waset, she could never recall if she heard her mother's name spoken by anyone else. Certainly, she would have heard her nearly always absent father or at least some of the other women of the household—or perhaps a servant or two—speak her mother's given name. But, no. Not to her memory. She tried imagining a name for her mother, but nothing seemed appropriate. For years she prayed to the Goddess for memory, but the prayer forever remained unanswered.

She recalled growing up later around a general feeling of dread and uncertainty and perhaps, she reasoned, that is why her mind chose most of the memories of her time with her mother to be good ones. Concern for the kingdom and fear of the Lower Kingdom's many invasions riddled her childhood memories as she listened to the women gossip in their chambers. The clearest memory of her mother, however, concerned the Goddess.

"You are a child of the Gift, Ramla," her mother always told her, taking Ramla's face in her hands and staring straight into her daughter's eyes. "Amunet, the Goddess of the Reeds, gave you the Gift. I knew this about you when you were born. Your eyes are so wide like mine, and they are beautiful because She gave you this Gift. They are brown like her rich soil. You are dedicated to Her. You can know things before they happen. But you must listen carefully to the Goddess when she speaks."

"Yes, mother," she would say, even though she didn't quite understand at the time exactly what her mother meant.

"And what does your name mean?" her mother would quiz her as she dried her hair by the river.

"Prophetess," Ramla would answer. That, she knew for sure.

"Never forget it," her mother would say, finishing the bath with a kiss of blessing on her head.

Ramla also knew enough to realize that she and her mother were part of the royal household and that brought with it both privileges and responsibilities. They were superior to many, perhaps, but all were in the shadow of the Great Lord.

As she grew, Ramla began to understand what her mother meant about her Gift. She would have a dream or experience a sensation about a person or thing, and the event would happen to that person. She once told the women that one of the king's wives would have twins, and the women laughed at her. When the woman did indeed have two boys, the women's laughter stopped and was replaced with wonder. She then told them that one of the boys would die of a sickness. When that happened, fear replaced wonder. Soon, the other women instructed their children to avoid the strange little girl with the large, dark eyes.

One of the younger women summoned her courage and asked her how she knew all of this. Ramla calmly replied that she didn't know for sure; all she knew was that the Goddess shared some things with her. The woman grew angry with Ramla, thinking that she was keeping something from her and simply wanted to keep the Gift to herself.

Thus Ramla grew into her eighth year as a lonely child. On her birthday that year, her mother took her to the Temple of the Goddess of the Reeds to offer a gift. The priest of the temple met them in the courtyard. "You must wait here," he said.

"But my daughter is gifted of the Goddess," Ramla's mother argued.

"I wasn't talking to your daughter," the priest said, and he took Ramla by the hand and led her inside the temple, leaving her mother outside. Ramla noticed the coolness of the ruddy-brown stones the moment they entered the lintel. Once her eyes adjusted to the dim light of the lamps, she looked up at the far wall and saw the Goddess Herself. She knew enough to not stare at the face of the Goddess, however.

The priest squeezed her hand. "Good!" he said. "You show no fear, but I can sense your awe and respect. Yes, truly; you are chosen by the Goddess."

Wordlessly, she looked up at the bald priest in his finery and heavy eye makeup. Her question needed no words, but he answered, "It is not usually allowed, but you can go up…" he said and held up a finger of warning before Ramla's face, "with respect."

He released her hand and Ramla, with her eyes downcast appropriately, walked heel to toe in a straight line to the base of the Goddess before her. Only then did she bow low respectfully. With her head against the coolness of the large stones, Ramla prayed, "Oh, Goddess! Do not hide from me! Protect me and my mother and your king. Thank you for your Gift, oh Great One!"

When she was finished with her prayer, Ramla raised her head and looked directly at the serene and stern face of the statue. A sense of peace and understanding entered her mind. At that moment, her union with the Goddess was broken as she heard the priest gasp loudly behind her. Ramla backed out from in front of the Goddess, and the priest met her at the back of the room and grabbed her roughly by the shoulders. "You looked at the Goddess in the face!" he cried, slapping her sharply across the cheek with the back of his hand. "You are cursed! Be gone with you!"

Ramla wriggled her shoulders from his grasp. "No, I am not cursed," she said, quietly as she rubbed her reddened cheek. "The Goddess is my friend," she explained. "She knows I meant no disrespect. She is my Goddess."

This affront was more than the poor man could bear. He took the wriggling girl by the arm and carried her out to her waiting mother. "Do not bring this blasphemer here again!" he ordered as he threw Ramla roughly to the ground at her mother's feet. Ramla began to cry quietly, and her mother narrowed her eyes at the priest.

"You are the blasphemer," Ramla's mother said. "You reject the one gifted by the Goddess Herself."

"Ah ha!" the man exclaimed. "I see where she gets it. You are each as bad as the other. I know who you are, daughter of Tjetjy! I shall see to it that he knows of your evil here today!"

"Don't bother," Ramla's mother said, gathering her child next to her side and turning to go. "I shall tell him myself."

Later, in their room, as they sat on the bed talking, Ramla's mother felt differently. She knew that some protocol had been broken and worried how it would affect them. Ramla comforted her mother. "Mother, all will be well. I know it. Listen to me. I saw it in the eyes of the Goddess after I spoke to Her. We do not need the temple to see the Goddess."

"What?"

"I said, we can see the Goddess anywhere. We can see any God anywhere. We have no need to go back to the temple again."

"No, my child," her mother said, shaking her head. "It is more than that. We have offended the priest. This is not good. He could make trouble for us. I don't know what will come of it, but it will not be good."

"Then I'm sorry, mother, that I have offended. I shall make it right."

"Ah, my darling," her mother said, drawing her close in a hug. "No, it is not in your control to make it right. You must do as the Goddess tells you. Never apologize for what a God tells you. That— that is beyond our control; yours, mine, and this ignorant priest's."

Aside from these memories, Ramla remembered little of what happened next. Separation from her mother happened to her, she surmised in later times, sometime in the next year or so; whether by death or the design of others she did not know. Then, a journey down the river followed—she recalled that much clearly—a journey made with other women and children she did not know. Mostly, her memory of the journey was that it was a trip filled with sadness. She would thank the Goddess later for keeping the deeper, more painful memories from her. Yet, during this time, Ramla had memories of hunger and of many tears. But through it all, she kept her dignity, and she kept her promises to her mother; she never forgot her name, and she never forgot her Gift.

TWO

A bram easily made the decision to go to Egypt. Nomads grew used to transition, even if the flocks grew large. In fact, the size of his herds made Abram's choice for him. His animals withered in the drought. And Egypt drew the dispossessed, the hungry, and the displaced like a well-watered, well-fed magnet. For most in that part of the world, it was better to live as a slave with a full belly than to starve a free man.

Yet, for Abram and his growing numbers of flocks and servants, Egypt could be simply like another stop on the journey for him and his half-sister/wife, Sarai. Then there was his nephew, Lot, and Lot's growing family and herds. Lot had been the only family that had stayed with Abram everyplace he had gone, but Abram knew that Lot's motivations were mostly selfish ones. Their place of birth, Ur, the land of their ancestors, seemed a lifetime ago. A move more north and west to the crossroads of Aram had followed after that.

The decision to go there was made by Abram's father, Terah. Then, after Terah's death, Abram picked up his entourage, and he and Lot moved to Canaan. That time, the choice had been Abram's but guided by the new God who revealed Himself to Abram as El. So, by that time, picking up everything and moving to Egypt seemed almost natural to Abram, even if El did not tell him to do so.

But the moves did not seem natural to Abram's wife. Sarai had been against all the moves from the start, at least passively. She didn't leave her relatives and the familiarity of Ur so easily. And she saw no reason to follow any God so capricious that He could not stay still.

And then there was the nephew, Lot, and his wife and daughters and servants and flocks. Lot, Abram thought, received neither wisdom nor joy from his father, a man Abram remembered well for having both. Thoughts of Lot and his poor, selfish decisions often caused Abram to sigh.

The messages from this new God had first come to Abram as he looked at his flocks on a clear, cool, breezy evening back in Aram. The message didn't frighten him, but it came as a strong yet calm voice, listing wonderful things that lay in the future: "A mighty people," the voice assured him he would become, and he would receive "protection from enemies." This God, El, also foretold he would be "a great nation," and, for Abram, at least, the most alluring and special was a new "land of promise." The old man had not questioned what this new God said would happen, but he didn't fully understand.

Why him? Why now? Why not when he was a much younger man?

"She'll not understand," Abram said to himself as he thought about having to tell his wife what the new God originally asked of him. His father, Terah, sprang from a long line of moon worshippers. In fact, several from his family had served the kings of Ur as astrologers for many generations.

Why would this new God—a God not only not worshipped by but also not known to Abram and his family—suddenly make Himself known in such a mysterious and powerful way as He did? These questions gnawed at Abram's heart daily.

"Take your family and go," the voice had said to Abram. "I'll show you a land that will be yours and your family's forever."

Abram had heard from the voice off and on since the time he was first told to move on that cool, clear evening. "That was, what, more than ten years ago?" Abram thought, counting the seasons in his head as he readied his wife for the news of the move to Egypt. They had made a semi-permanent home in Bethel—the place name meaning "House of El," a name given to it by Abram—and Abram knew that his wife would not want to uproot and move yet again.

But not much had been heard from the new God lately. "No, Sarai will not be pleased," the old man considered. She thought their wanderings were over when they had reached Aram. But no; the New God brought more upheaval after that. Bethel had finally offered a bit of stability, and the nearby woods provided fuel and sustenance, but only up to a point. As for his nephew, Lot, he didn't mind anything. Lot simply did as he was told—as long as it benefitted him or his family.

And now this. Egypt. Drought leading to famine leading to yet another move. If the new God could keep His promises, then why could He not end the famine? At least that was the argument Abram thought his wife would make. Yet Abram did not always doubt. In his heart of hearts, he trusted that El would not see him this far only to abandon him now.

When he entered Sarai's tent, he saw her head rise up from her sewing to meet his eyes. Despite being almost eighty, Sarai's beauty still stirred Abram's heart. He would often stare at her for long periods, amazed that she bore little signs of age. She'd even kept her teeth. Her dark brown hair still showed no streaks of gray or silver. Abram always noticed the faces of visitors when they saw Sarai. A lesser man might have been jealous of the way other men looked at his wife, but Abram wasn't. He took it as a badge of honor that they, to a person, recognized great beauty when they saw it.

"I've been with the animals," he began, then his voice trailed off. Sarai closed her eyes to listen as if she couldn't bear the words. Not having to look directly into her eyes allowed Abram to find his nerve again. "We must move them, and soon."

Sarai knew what that meant. "Egypt," she said, flatly. Abram wasn't surprised. Of course, she was no fool; Egypt had food for the animals and for them. And water. Always water. It was not unlike Ur in that regard.

He nodded. The look of anger Abram expected from his wife's face never materialized. Instead, Sarai responded with an incredible sadness around her eyes, and this broke Abram's heart. He could deal with her temper—that, he was used to.

This sadness, however, was new lately. It threw him off balance; he could never handle Sarai's sadness well. Compounding her sorrow was the fact that she could not provide a child for her beloved if slightly odd husband. Yet, none of this diminished the love the couple shared.

Sarai lowered her head to her chest. "If you think it best, my good husband," she said, finally, flatly, her eyes returning to her sewing.

"Good husband," Sarai had said. The words stung sharper than if she had openly rebuked him. Abram turned and went outside quickly before Sarai could see his tears. She looked through the tent opening as Abram departed, and the thought crossed her mind that once they left she might never see Bethel's hills again.

THREE

Ramla's next clear memory came from the upper Nile town of Shashotep. Along with the other women and children, she was herded off the boat at the city dock and into a nearby, makeshift enclosure of rough-cut wood slats.

A saying in Egypt was that if you wanted anything, you could always get it in Shashotep. Shashotep was the middle city that straddled the shifting front lines between the warring and divided Upper Kingdom and the Lower Kingdom. Sometimes one side or another would make forays into the other's area and temporarily take over the city. For the most part, however, both sides recognized the benefit of having a neutral, go-between area where trading could take place despite their differences.

As an open city, Shashotep bustled with trade. Most of the trading these days was in human merchandise as the wars between the South and North had reached a temporary stalemate. Representatives of both pharaohs, the Upper and Lower, could be found there at any given time. Most of the time, that meant slave traders.

Apparently, Ramla had been marked as one the slavers from the north might have a special interest in. A dab of red paint had been put on her left arm at some point in the journey, and she had received plenty of food and care on the boat journey north despite being with the others. Some of the women and children, she remembered, eyed her enviously. Ramla remembered trying to rub off the red paint, but she couldn't remove it all.

A day after they arrived, a gaunt but finely dressed man with heavily drawn eyes came to the enclosure to view the captives, led by a short, stocky man with red hair around his ears who had accompanied them on the journey. "Are you certain she was of the household?" Ramla heard the gaunt man ask as they approached the group.

"Yes, my lord; I am sure of it. The one who sold her to me assured me so."

"The word of a trader?" the gaunt man snorted. "Worthless!"

The red-haired man, afraid of losing the sale, ignored the insult. "Ah, you will see. She has breeding."

The two stopped at the enclosure directly in front of Ramla. The group around her drew back, but Ramla remained almost defiantly in place. She looked from the eyes of one man to the eyes of the next.

"See! I told you. Bearing. Breeding. Anyone can see it," Redhead exclaimed.

"Are you saying I cannot?" the gaunt man said accusingly.

"No, no, my lord Tefibi. I meant no disrespect, only…"

"Only that what you see as bearing could be ignorance in one so young or even insolent pride, and that will not do."

"No, of course not, my lord," Redhead agreed apologetically.

The gaunt man put a hand to his chin and rubbed. Ramla still stood her ground and continued to look at both men. Finally, the gaunt man said, "Yes. I will take the chance, Hanya. You usually have a good eye for these things, even if I am loathe to admit it."

Redhead turned his hands over in anticipation of the money he was about to receive, but the deal was not done yet. "At my price?" he asked.

"No; in that I will not bend. Twenty is my final offer."

Now it was Redhead's turn to rub his chin. "Yes. Agreed. If you will take more of the chattel behind her."

"Agreed," the gaunt man said with a tired sigh. He managed to give Ramla a secret, quick smile that only she saw before he turned away. And with that, Ramla soon found herself on another boat headed still farther north, farther downstream from her past.

Somewhere along this journey, the gaunt man came to Ramla and to the slave woman who had been ordered to take care of her. "What is your name?" he demanded. Ramla, again showing no fear, answered. The man cocked his head when she said it, and he nodded slightly as if he recognized the significance of the meaning. Satisfied, he said, "My name is Tefibi. I serve the Great King, My Lord Merikare in his city of Nen-Nesu. You will serve him there, too." He added, "If you are found to be worthy to do so."

"Yes," Ramla replied.

"Yes…?" Tefibi said, waiting for Ramla to use proper courtesy.

"Yes, my lord," Ramla said.

"Better. And don't forget it." Tefibi added. "Now," he continued,

"Tell me; were you truly a member of the household or is that tale only invented to make me pay more for you?"

"Truly," Ramla said. "My mother and I were of the family of a great man of the Great Lord of Two Lands in Waset."

"And yet, you have the name of someone who serves in a temple. Can you explain that?" Tefibi asked.

Ramla's heart decided that this man meant her no harm, but she understood it was important to him to find out about her. So, she looked deeply into Tefibi's eyes. After a pause, she said, "Sir, how is your wife's mother? Is she still sick?"

Tefibi raised his head and looked at the river bank. His eyes darted back and forth in thought. "How did you know she was sick?" he asked. Then he looked back down at Ramla's dark, large eyes. "Ah, I see. You have been gifted by the Goddess. I have met others like you. Most of them are men, however. In a woman, it is rare. In a girl, even more so."

"She has blessed me, yes," Ramla said.

"I understand you," Tefibi said, as he reached out to touch Ramla's dark hair. But he stopped his hand just above her head. Instead, he patted the air above her. "Let's keep this between us, shall we? I make you a promise, Ramla, that I will protect you. If you have need, ask me."

"I speak about these things only when the Goddess instructs me to do so, sir," Ramla answered.

"You have answered well, my child," Tefibi said, almost with affection.

FOUR

Tefibi made good on his promise to Ramla. For the remainder of the short trip, he made sure she had everything she needed. When the boat arrived at Nen-Nesu, he personally escorted her to the king's house. Usually that job was given to an underling, but Tefibi had been thinking about the small girl with the large, dark eyes. They had spoken several times over the past two days, and every time they spoke Tefibi came away from the conversation impressed with her gift, her poise, her composure and her pride.

Yes, this was a rare child. He, a man who had for years seen so many children come and go as slaves through the flesh markets of both Upper and Lower Egypt, now felt a connection of some sort with this child. He and his wife had not been blessed with children; would it be impious, no, would it be disloyal to the king to wish that they could have this unusual girl Ramla as their own?

But how could he do it? He himself was a trusted yet still relatively minor official in charge of procurement for Merikare. Only once had he even been in the presence of the Great King. And when Ramla would be turned over to the eunuch in charge of the king's service to begin her training, protocol would prevent Tefibi from ever having any contact with her. As they were about to cross the door into the outer room of the chief eunuch's courtyard, Tefibi's senses left him.

He took Ramla by the shoulders and knelt before her. Almost eye to eye, he looked into the girl's face and said, quietly but sternly, "Listen…!" But no other words came. How could he feel such strong emotion for a girl, a slave, whom he had only met a few days earlier? Yet, he could see that Ramla, too, was touched; her moist eyes smiled weakly at him, and she nodded in acknowledgement of things he did not need to say with words.

This time, Tefibi allowed himself to pat her on the head, turn her around, and wordlessly send her out of his life and through the great, metal-covered wooden door into the world of King Merikare's great palace. He watched her go and silently offered a prayer to the Goddess on her behalf.

Ramla's life then settled into a routine for some weeks. From the stewards she received training, daily, on household protocol and service. Girls her age and a bit older were still too young for the harem, but they were prized as personal servants of the royal families in both parts of Egypt. She knew well of such girls back in her home in Upper Egypt and as a younger child had watched them. It confused her at the time as to why she could not play with them, but her mother quickly taught her the what even if she did not understand the why.

Protocol and service and being around fine objects and the daily life of a palace had been bred into her, so she quickly distinguished herself among the other girls. Nights were spent in the room with several of the other girls. There, she could cover her face and shed the tears for her lost mother and her lost life in Waset. Rumors of her Gift preceded her, which meant that Tifibi must somehow have informed the chief eunuch of how special Ramla was. Again, most of the girls and the women and eunuchs kept their distance unless they wanted to know something about a family member or their own good or bad fortunes.

As for her Gift, the feelings she had remained like a dull sensation in her chest, but she heard from the Goddess less and less. She had learned that while people often wished to hear what would happen to them as the Goddess revealed it to her, she also learned that they often resented it when they learned it. So, Ramla daily became less aware of the Gift and concentrated on becoming more efficient in what to do and when to do it and to whom, and so she often kept to herself, much as she had when she was even younger in Waset. Still, she never forgot her mother's admonitions.

Five years passed.

A quiet child turned into a lovely young girl in the service of Merikare's household. Soon, because of her quick mind, she was tasked with taking care of the women of visiting dignitaries from other lands near and far, caring for their hair and assisting with the baths, helping them with court protocol and teaching them how to bow before the throne of the Great King. In this capacity, Ramla, with her quick mind, became knowledgeable in several languages and came to understand at least some words in almost every tongue known to Merikare's court.

If a special dignitary visited with a retinue of women, Ramla would quickly be able to discern which one of them carried the most importance among the visitors and would inform the chief steward, who would, in turn, announce the visitors in that order. Perhaps this gift, too, was from the Goddess. This ability served to impress more than a few visitors to Nen-Nesu.

And so one day, when a foreign, wealthy older woman and her brother, another younger male relative, and their servants were brought into the household, it fell to Ramla to be assigned the task of taking care of this older woman. The household rumor was that this woman was to be another bride of the great Pharaoh Merikare.

FIVE

In the train of the pack animals, Sarai rode astride the donkey led by Abram. Certainly, he could entrust the job to a servant, but he wanted to be there if and when his wife needed anything. For Abram, it was his pride to do so.

Crossing the coastal area from Canaan into the Sinai and over towards Egypt, the large group of animals and servants moved slowly every day, but having the sea breezes during the days and evenings made the trip more endurable. Ships would pass going each way to and from Canaan, and the younger among them would wave excitedly at first. After a few days, most grew tired of the game, and everyone simply wanted to arrive in Egypt.

The movement of such a large group of people and animals became noticed early in the journey. Lot's herders never seemed to control the flock and were always having to range far and wide to gather the stragglers, so their presence became much easier to detect in any case. Outriders from Egypt showed up before Abram's group arrived in Sinai. They demanded to know what business the group had in Egypt, and Abram informed everyone to be honest if asked or to send them back to him or his chief servant, Eliezer. The outriders seemed to be satisfied with the answers they received and rode back the way they came.

Then, only three days from Egypt, a larger group appeared. Abram put together a fete for them at the seaside since it was near evening and the group had set up camp for the night. It became known that the entourage from Egypt was from the pharaoh's household, so Abram's decision to feast with the men proved fortunate.

As the sun began setting over their shoulders into the sea, everyone sat down in a large semicircle facing Abram's tents. When the first courses were brought up, Sarai came out of the tent and sat at Abram's right hand as was their custom. Her appearance caused a stir among the Egyptians, and they began nodding to each other as if in approval or confirmation of some sort.

"Your wife…she is beautiful," the captain of the Egyptian band said to Abram as he motioned to Sarai with fingers syrupy from the tray of figs and sweetmeat that lay before him. "The stories we have heard of her beauty are true," he added. That meant the earlier outriders had made a report on these nomads as they made their way closer to Egypt.

"She is also my sister," Abram said with a laugh, trying to explain more to these representatives of the pharaoh. This news seemed to make the captain take more interest in Sarai for some reason. The translator, one of the Egyptians, either did not hear or did not translate that Abram had said "also." The captain kept asking why Sarai had not married since even at her age she was so beautiful. Abram sat up straighter and was about to correct the misconception.

But Sarai understood the cause of confusion and stopped Abram by touching his arm. She whispered, "Wait; if they didn't understand that you are also my husband, they may be more favorable towards us!" Abram understood and nodded. He allowed the Egyptian captain to continue to speak. Soon, he saw that perhaps Sarai's instinct was right.

"The Great King Merikare is one who appreciates beauty, no matter its origins," the captain explained. "Such a one as this would make an excellent wife for the king. We shall go tomorrow and tell the household of your coming!" he promised.

The next morning, after his men woke and tended to their animals, the Egyptian captain led his men away back towards Egypt, carrying with him the news that a great beauty was soon to arrive at the court of the Great King.

Sarai considered it a triumph. "He must give us what we need, my husband, if he thinks I am a prospective wife." Abram did not share her optimism. "My wife," Abram said to Sarai later that day, "what will happen to us if the Great King finds out we have been less than truthful with him?"

Sarai smiled. "My husband, don't you always say that El will provide?"

SIX

"Princess!" Ramla thought derisively. This woman would not know what it was to be a princess if she lived in Egypt for 1,000 years. Her loud voice, the uncouth way she carried herself—no, this woman was no princess. How could the Merikare think to add her as a wife? Surely, Sarai's introduction before the great king was an embarrassment to the court. Ramla turned her nose up at the smell of livestock that now seemed to be in everything the woman owned. It permeated her hair, and it seemed that she even put the milk of the animals on her skin!

As she unpacked the newcomer's belongings and laid them out on the bed, Ramla thought of how she could remove the offensive smelling items without hurting the older woman's feelings and not spread the raw odor throughout all the rooms. Maybe she could teach this woman a thing or two subtly. Surely Merikare would not want such foul-smelling clothes on one of his wives!

Ramla ran her fingers across the hem of one of the garments. The cloth itself was fine, certainly, but the tailor obviously had little talent. There was no art in it. Coarse threads at the garment's edge testified to this fact. Ramla smiled a wise smile. The fabric mirrored the owner—crude work made out of something potentially lovely.

Yes, Ramla could not deny that there was a rustic beauty about the older woman. Her features were indeed comely, her face one of a woman decades younger. Even though she did not want to admit it, she began to understand why Merikare took her as a wife. He collected all things of beauty, and Sarai was only another of those things. Yet, such rude behavior in a wife seemed out of place in the life and household of a pharaoh, Ramla thought.

"Here!" a sharp voice sounded behind her. It was Sarai, and she had entered the room to find the servant with her hands on a favorite dress. "Are you trying to steal from me?" the older woman said accusingly. Ramla was shocked into quietness, taken aback at the older woman's accusation. She dropped the dress on the bed as this Princess continued.

"Don't touch my things!" she commanded.

"Steal… Steal your things?" Ramla asked incredulously. "Mistress, I would never!" She said.

"You can't deny it!" Sarai said. "I know what I saw! My husband will know of this thing."

Ramla's mind raced. She instantly imagined what Merikare would say to this accusation if he heard of it. Would he cast her out of the palace—or worse?

"Yes, my husband Abram will not put up with theft," Sarai said angrily, pushing past Ramla at the bed and gathering her clothes in her arms.

"What?" Ramla asked, suddenly realizing the magnitude of what she had heard. "What did you say?" she asked in a tone that was anything but subservient. The older woman, realizing that she had revealed more than she should have, tried to cover her mistake. "I meant my brother," she said hastily. "My brother Abram will surely know of this." And she busied herself by rolling up her crude clothes and putting them in the rough canvas bag from which they came. "You need to mind your own business," Sarai said. "And don't take that tone with me," she added.

Ramla began to realize that she needed to pretend she had heard nothing revealing, yet she also sensed that she had been let in on a great secret. "Yes," Ramla bowed, "I will do as my mistress asks with great joy. It is my wish to serve and please," she said, reverting to the subservient tone. "I was only trying to help my mistress by unpacking her things," she explained. "I am fully capable of doing that myself," Sarai said sharply. "You may go now," the older woman ordered.

"Yes, mistress. I am here to make you happy. I am close by if you have need." Ramla bowed and remained bent over as she backed her way out of the room. Outside, against the cool outer wall next to the door, Ramla put her back on the wall and slid down it until she sat on her haunches. She thought about what she had heard. "So, they are not brother and sister," she thought and nodded. "They are husband and wife."

SEVEN

As was the custom, Merikare and Sarai sat next to each other at the wedding feast as they and their guests enjoyed the food and drink. Course after course was presented before them, and all the while dancers, jugglers, musicians, and animals from all corners of Egypt came and went as entertainment.

Ramla stayed close to Sarai, assisting her with the different plates and cups as they were brought. She tried her best to explain to Sarai what the different dishes were, but the older woman didn't seem to care and barely ate from her plates as the courses were brought before her. The woman had refused to wear most of the Egyptian finery that Ramla had laid out for her; instead, she insisted on wearing her own garments, and acquiesced only in wearing some of the make-up provided. Still, Ramla thought, she was a beauty.

Ramla also kept an eye on the man, Abram. As the brother of the bride and the brother-in-law of the pharaoh, Abram occupied the seat of honor next to his sister-wife on the other side of Sarai. He and Sarai often put their heads together in whispers. Merikare did not seem to either notice or mind.

As she went about her work, Ramla tried to hear what the two were saying, but she could only make out a few words. To anyone else, it looked as if brother and sister were talking about the wedding feast. But knowing what she knew, Ramla saw a deeper meaning. She was suddenly filled with the idea that the deception she knew to be perpetrated by these two foreigners was made more out of fear than to truly try to deceive. That did not make it better, she thought, but it did help explain it in her mind.

It was also the first time that Ramla took a good look at this Abram. He seemed much older than Sarai, but he had a kindness about his eyes that the woman lacked. To her, he seemed like a gentle grandfather. She noticed that, like his wife, his clothes were of fine material but constructed in a crude fashion. The man Abram's appearance and frame were not unbecoming for one of his age; he seemed to still have most of his teeth and his cheeks bore no sign of wrinkles. She also noticed that Abram moved, even seated, as if he still had his coordination and flexibility, something that often left a man of advanced age.

But Ramla's perceptions drew her deeper into Abram's face. As she studied him, she suddenly felt a kinship—something that she had not felt for some time, something that she feared had left her long ago—a feeling that here, at last, was someone else connected to the world of the Gods. The conversation between Abram and Sarai brought her out of her thoughts.

Ramla was also able to tell by the way that the pair talked to each other in their hushed tones that there was great affection between them that went beyond the usual relationship between brother and sister. There was a physical yet non-touching intimacy that their looks at each other and their interacting body language betrayed. So, watching them, she became convinced in her mind that what she had been led to believe was true; these two were actually husband and wife.

As the feast continued, the younger relative of Abram, the nephew, Lot, who sat with his family on the opposite side of the feast from the married couple, came to be increasingly boisterous from drink. He began offering loud, boisterous opinions about the different performers who came before them in the great hall. Most of his comments were crude and certainly inappropriate, Ramla thought, as she cleared another set of plates from before Sarai. He often referred to his wife, a small and light-skinned woman with a protruding jawline, in his vile comments.

Ramla managed to hear Sarai say to Abram, "I wish he would not drink so much."

Without bothering to whisper, Abram answered back, "We are not used to drinking this much. I'm afraid Lot likes the beer more than he should."

At that moment, with a loud cry, the young man Lot decided to stand up and hurl a piece of bread at one of the monkeys that had been brought in to perform. Lot's wife giggled and clapped her hands in delight at her husband's antics. Two of the other monkeys grabbed at the bread, which caused Lot to break off an even bigger chunk of a loaf and throw it at the animals. The poor trainer was helpless to stop it. The act quickly descended into chaos as other monkeys started fighting each other for the bread. All of this caused

Lot to laugh even louder as he came around the table and started imitating the dancing monkeys.

Ramla looked at Merikare. She knew what the furrowed brows meant. Soon, everyone could see that he was displeased. The musicians stopped their accompaniment simply because no one watched them any longer. A loud murmur of disappointment grew among the wedding guests as the only movement on the floor was of the squabbling monkeys led by this drunken, dancing foreigner.

The pharaoh gave a slight nod to his chief steward, and the baldheaded man strode forward. "The Great King Merikare and his new bride thank you all for coming," he announced. Sarai looked at Marikare, but he did not look at her. She then turned to Abram. Abram shrugged his shoulders as if to say he didn't know what was happening. Without a word to Sarai, Marikare stood up and strode quickly out of the room followed by his bodyguards.

"What...is that it?" Sarai asked to no one. She began loudly berating Lot for his antics. "This is all your fault, you drunken fool!" she yelled. Lot's wife shot a look of anger towards Sarai, but the older woman didn't see it. Ramla took it upon herself to interrupt softly and whisper to Sarai, "My mistress, the wedding feast is finished."

Sarai quickly turned her head away from Ramla's whisper. "I was not addressing you!" Sarai snapped. Her harsh tone echoed in the chamber as the wedding guests silently made their way out of the great hall. Lot, noticing that people were leaving, stopped his monkey dance and slurred, "Wait...where is everybody going?"

It was not enough that this crude woman had been made the wife of the Great King, or that the drunken young relative had made a mockery of the wedding celebration. Being publicly embarrassed like that wounded Ramla's pride deeply. The red of embarrassment glowed under and through her brown skin. As Sarai and Abram made their way out of the hall to their respective rooms, Ramla followed Sarai, her face burning with shame.

The servants who stayed behind to clean up from the wedding feast remarked as they worked that the events of that evening were certainly a bad omen for the new union.

EIGHT

T he skin lesions started on Merikare's back. They mystified his doctors. The physicians searched the tablets and scrolls in the archives, looking for symptoms, causes, cures, all to no avail. No remedy seemed to help, and the blisters spread along with the King's pain. Soon, other members of the household started exhibiting the same symptoms. Animals were sacrificed. The best seers in the kingdom consulted with each other.

Finally, a consensus was reached. Someone in the King's household had offended Osiris, and atonement was called for. It was impolitic to blame the King directly, and the wise men learned to cast a general net of suspicion upon the household rather than on the throne itself. Any wise king would search his own heart to see if he had offended; any unwise king could resent a direct accusation and seek vengeance on any who might malign him.

Soon, everyone in the household began whispering about and theorizing as to the cause of the malady that lay on the head of the Great King. Ramla took no part in the palace gossip, but she felt in her heart that she knew the reason for the plague. It would be disloyal for her not to reveal it, she thought. No, more than disloyal; it would be ungrateful to the Great King for her not to tell what she knew about these nomads who had brought such disgrace to the palace. But whom to tell? It would have to be an official high enough that word could get to Merikare, but it could not be someone so high that protocol would prohibit Ramla from speaking to him directly about the situation in detail. She prayed to the Goddess for wisdom. The answer soon presented itself.

"How is the comfort of the Great King's new wife, Ramla?" the Chief Steward asked her one day as they passed in the hallway outside of Sarai's rooms. The interaction was somewhat unusual, as an official of the household of such a rank would usually ask a lower chamberlain to inquire. Ramla sensed that the Chief Steward was fishing for information, and that he, aware of the gift she bore from the Goddess, had been sent to divine what Ramla might know.

"My task is one of joy, sir," she said, not wanting the man to think her petty for speaking ill of Sarai, even though working for the older woman was perhaps the most difficult task Ramla had yet faced in her time at the palace.

The Chief Steward paused. He moved closer to Ramla and whispered, "Come, come; we both know that these people are not like us. I know that the Great King's new wife is a shrew."

Ramla tried not to reveal what she was thinking. "Oh, sir," she began, "I…it's…my work is not difficult, sir."

The Chief Steward bit his lower lip with impatience. "You cannot say that, Ramla. I may not be in these halls often, but I know what goes on in the house of the Great King. Tell me what you are thinking."

So Ramla told him what she knew, what she had seen, and what she had heard. The man closed his eyes, tilted his head back, and sighed deeply. He realized that he had found what he was looking for. "Have you told anyone else what you know?" he asked. She shook her head. "Good," he said. "I charge you; do not tell a soul what you have told me. I will take care of this. Thank you, Ramla," he said as he left. "I will not forget your loyalty to the Great King." Ramla felt a sense of calm and satisfaction as the man strode away. She knew it would only be a matter of time before the Great King would rid himself of this petty lower-caste woman and her brother/husband.

Merikare could not shed the nomads quickly enough. A high-ranking steward was dispatched to Abram's room with the message that he and his household were to gather their belongings and leave Egypt immediately. So that no one would lose face, the Great King magnanimously gave Abram several small chests of jewels and gold, spices and perfumes. Sheep and goats and donkeys, too. And servants, the chamberlain added.

There was one servant in particular who carried special value, the man explained to Abram. The young woman who waited upon Abrams wife/sister, a servant named Ramla, who was known to process special abilities endowed by the gods, was to accompany Abram's family as they left. "And," the servant added as he left, "you understand that you are never to return to this land." Abram nodded rapidly in agreement.

Ramla was speechless when she heard the news. At first, she thought she had misheard, and then she tried to use grasping bits of logic to think that maybe the Great King meant she was supposed to accompany the nomads until they left the territory and then she could return to the Great King's house and to her duties. But no, apparently it was true that she had been given to them permanently, like the chests of precious items and the donkeys and the goats and lambs. It saddened her even more when she gathered her belongings and no one from the Great King's household, none of the women or any other servants, bothered to stop by to say farewell to her or wish for her a blessing from the Gods.

Ramla could barely keep her composure when she joined Abram's caravan in the large outer courtyard of the palace before departure. The enclosure was filled with Abram's family and servants, all talking loudly and rapidly, shouting over each other as they organized their places in the caravan. Lot, the nephew, shouted orders to servants and to his wife, almost simultaneously, and seemed to be going over a list of new and luxurious items the family had obtained in Egypt, making sure that he left with his share of the loot. Such a raucous display as this she found distasteful.

Ramla spotted Abram near the gate and was immediately struck by the fact that he seemed so calm in the middle of all the chaos. He gave a thin smile when he spotted her over the crowd and waved her to him with one hand. She pressed her way through the throng, her sack of belongings jostling as she moved through the crowd. "Ah, El be praised, so, you have found us," Abram said to her. It was the first thing he had ever said to her directly. Ramla saw that he stood next to a donkey, on which Sarai sat. The older woman made it a point to not look at Ramla. It was as if she resented the fact that Abram spoke to the younger woman at all.

Another older man, a man Ramla had never seen before, suddenly stood on a wooden box and yelled to the large group. "Listen!" he boomed. The crowd obviously knew him and hushed quickly. Even Lot stopped his inventory and looked at the man. "We will leave and head north to the Coast Road. Make sure you stay with your group. Stragglers will not be looked for!" He paused in his speech and looked directly at Lot when he said this part.

"Yes, we heard you, Eliezer," Lot yelled back, annoyed that his group had been singled out.

To the rest of the crowd the older man continued. "We must make haste," he thundered. Then, looking up to the sentries on the wall, he yelled, "Open the gates!"

The large double wooden doors, covered in a thin layer of gilt, swung wide on their well-oiled hinges as the chains that moved them rattled loudly. The rattling was quickly drowned out by the great groan of movement through the gates of the large number of Abram's caravan leaving the courtyard.

From a high window above the melee below, the Chief Steward placed a meaty hand on his bald head as he watched the throng begin to stream out of the Merikare's palace. "I'm sorry, Ramla, please forgive me" he said to himself, and made a sign of luck as he turned away from the window. "I couldn't take the risk that you would tell someone else what you knew and embarrass the Great King."

Out loud and to no one, he added, "May the Goddess bless you."

NINE

Sarai rode on her donkey near the front of the great caravan, and Abram insisted on walking every step by her side. Ramla was given a donkey of her own, and she was told to ride slightly behind her new mistress in case any assistance was needed. Her animal carried water and items Sarai might need during the trip.

Ramla's heart sank even lower when she saw the great white sides of the three glorious pyramids, the sun reflecting mightily off the tombs, get smaller and smaller behind her as the caravan made its way north and east. She kept turning around on her animal to see what she was leaving behind. Ramla had not felt this way since she was first made captive those years ago. She was adrift. The humiliation of following these uncouth nomads, of having to be their permanent servant, she felt, was the worst possible punishment one could bear. She wondered which God she had angered that would bring her such ignominy. Perhaps, she thought, the God that Abram invoked as he greeted her, this El-God, had cursed her. Perhaps the old crone, Sarai, had brought the God's wrath on her.

A man who introduced himself as Eliezer, a man whose skin was more olive colored compared to her dark flesh, explained to her over the course of the first few nights when the caravan stopped what was required of her and what services the new mistress might need. This Eliezer was the man with the loud voice who had ordered the caravan to move in the Great King's outer courtyard the day they left; he seemed to be the nomads' equivalent of a chief steward and business manager rolled into one. Ramla came to know that he was from the ancient city of Damascus, and her experience in the great king's court had given her a working knowledge of that city's language. So, she and Eliezer spoke freely to each other.

Despite this connection, Eliezer's orders for Ramla came in short, direct, unemotional sentences. Perhaps, she thought, this simplicity and directness is what made him a good business manager, someone Abram trusted with everything he possessed.

"She likes warm milk at bedtime. She will wear the same clothes for many days. Then she will discard them. Leave the tent when Abram enters it." And so on. Much of it involved practical matters, but there was no formality or grace to the functions as Ramla was trained for and used to back in Egypt. "You will not need your Egyptian makeup," he informed her. It is not our way. He also gave her the longer, thicker garments like what the other women of the group wore that included a head covering. "Give your old clothes over to me. You are one of us, now." This last statement by Eliezer felt like a dagger to Ramla's heart.

It was also through Eliezer that Ramla first understood about Abram's God, El. "You need to know about the master's God. He calls him El. Abram will not make a move without consulting him."

At this Ramla spoke up. She recalled Abram's invocation of this God in the courtyard before they left. "As it should be," she said, looking at Eliezer directly.

Eliezer looked up and at the horizon. He narrowed his eyes and said, "Yes, as it should be." He went on to explain, in a few sentences, the history of the past few years. "It is important that you know this," he said, in conclusion. "You will understand more as you see it." His explanation caused Ramla to conclude that this El was not a vengeful God and thus was not the reason for her predicament.

Ramla was given a small bedroll and pillow, and Eliezer directed her to a corner of Sarai's tent. "That is your area," he said matter-of-factly. From there, Ramla endured the first two nights of hearing the old woman snore louder than anyone she had ever heard before. During her wakefulness, Ramla pondered her options. She could, with very little effort, run away and go back to Egypt. It would be better than staying here, she reasoned.

At first, Sarai barely acknowledged Ramla's presence, not even a nod when Ramla helped her with the meals or prepared the bedclothes. The first time Sarai spoke to her at all was when she yelled at Ramla for not having water ready in the evening. "You have been told what I require!" shrieked Sarai the third evening away from Egypt. Ramla, with bowed head, motioned with an open hand to the waiting ewer of water and cloth. The older woman had simply failed to see it. Sarai took this action as impudence. "Can you not speak? Are you mute as well as stupid?" Sarai ranted.

Abram entered the tent at that moment. Ramla moved to leave with a slight bow as she had been instructed. Abram had obviously heard the raised voice of his wife from outside because he asked, with seemed innocence, "How is everything, my wife?"

Sarai ignored Abram's question and yelled at Ramla to stop. "You don't leave when I'm talking to you!" she said. Ramla, with her eyes cast down, turned to face her mistress. Sarai then addressed Abram. "She is worse than useless," Sarai said to her husband. "She can't get anything right."

For a moment Abram didn't answer. "My wife," he said finally, licking his lips as he sought the correct words, "what is it you wish?"

"I want her to do her job. Is that too much to ask?" Sarai spat. "Some great gift the Great King gave us!" she added sarcastically.

Abram nodded thoughtfully. He turned to Ramla and said, "Is there anything you need that will help you serve my wife?"

Ramla allowed herself to look up at Abram, and she searched his face. Again, she saw a kindness there, but she also became aware that the man's relationship with his wife was deeply complicated. She decided to swallow her pride and apologize, if only to please him and not Sarai.

"No, master," Ramla said softly. "I have been lacking in my job. I ask the forgiveness of my mistress and of you, sir."

"There!" Abram replied, turning to his wife. "You see, all is well. She will try to do better." Sarai seemed less convinced, but she pursed her lips and made a "harrumph" sound which Ramla took to mean, "We will see."

"Thank you, Ramla," Abram said, turning back to the young woman. "You may go now." Ramla exited the tent, but she stayed near the flap so she could hear.

"She thinks she is so special," the old woman said. "Just because she is from Egypt doesn't mean that she is better than we are. I will not have a servant who looks down on me as she does."

Even through the tent flap, Ramla could hear Abram sigh heavily. "I'm sure she doesn't feel that way," he said soothingly. "She has been trained to do things a certain way. You cannot expect her to learn our way so quickly. Please be patient, my wife."

Part of what Sarai said was true. It pained Ramla somewhat that she felt as she did, but, because of the attitude of the older woman, Ramla did not feel as bad as she might otherwise. The thought crossed her mind that the one she served was not Sarai; the one she served was the Goddess.

Ramla listened to the couple argue for a few moments until she didn't want to listen anymore. She reached up and tore off her head covering and walked away from the tent and into the darkness outside of the camp. She missed the freedom of movement of the lighter-weighted clothing of her home. These confining clothes mirrored her feelings of being trapped and miserable.

The great band of stars hung above her like a glittering arch in the night sky. Ramla looked up and followed a shooting star as it moved towards the dark horizon. "Oh, Goddess," she said aloud, "I pray that you will guide me and give me wisdom. Do not hold your words from my heart. I know you are there. Tell me what to do." A breeze swirled around her suddenly, and Ramla felt comforted, as if the presence of the Goddess herself had come to her in the wind.

After her prayer, Ramla returned to the tent. She paused at the entrance to make sure that Abram had gone. From inside the tent, she could hear Sarai beginning to snore softly. She entered and made her way to her corner bed roll, dousing the olive oil lamp on her way. Soon after lying down, and despite the increasingly loud snoring of the older woman, Ramla slept. A great serenity had come upon her. She had reached a decision. She would run away.

TEN

"She is often missing for long stretches at a time. I know that one day she will up and run away. I simply know it," Sarai said. Then, imitating Ramla's Egyptian accent in derision, Sarai mimicked, "But mistress, I am only taking a walk when I go out."

Abram felt that his dear wife was being childish, but he had suspected for some time that Sarai harbored jealousy of the young woman. At that moment, Ramla entered the tent. "There she is now!" Sarai teased angrily. "There you are, you little runaway! Hagar!" Sarai exclaimed suddenly, using the Chaldean word for the action. "Hagar! That's what you are! That's who you are! Hagar! Run back to your master in Egypt!" She shook a fist at Ramla.

Ramla blushed with guilt. She had indeed been scouting the route the caravan had taken to see how far she could get before her absence would be noticed. She was also trying to remember where the watering holes and wells dotted the way they had come.

"Be calm, my wife," Abram said in more of a request than an order. "See? She is here. Ramla isn't going anywhere. Are you, Ramla?" Abram looked at the young woman searchingly. He suspected the truth and asked the question to ensure that she would reconsider her choice and stay with them.

"As you say, master," Ramla answered. Abram noticed her evasiveness.

"No, no, you are here with us. This is your home, now. See, my wife? She is staying." Abram nodded to Ramla for reassurance, but Ramla remained impassive. "At least she is not lying simply to please me," Abram thought approvingly.

But the nickname Sarai gave Ramla became the only name Sarai would use to address her. "Hagar, where's my sash? Hagar, why are you so slow? Hagar…Hagar…Hagar…" It angered Ramla every time she heard it, but she could not openly deny it and be truthful. So, she bore the nickname in silence. This angered her more and more as the days wore on, and it increased the tension between the two women.

The caravan of animals, servants, shepherds, and family made its way slowly north and then east into the Negev, back towards Bethel and the land El had promised to Abram. News from groups headed towards Egypt told the group that the famine in the land had subsided somewhat, that rain had soaked the ground in the past few weeks and that the year's grass seemed promising. "El be praised!" Abram exclaimed when Eliezer gave him the news. Even Sarai managed a wan smile when she heard.

When they returned to Bethel, Abram gave word that the group would camp for many days as he would offer sacrifices to El. Ramla managed to slip away from Sarai's tent and found a place within hearing of Abram's sacrificial altar. She sat cross-legged and watched, fascinated at Abram and his servants as they prepared the wood and the animals. Abram noticed her presence and nodded to her in recognition, but he did not tell her to leave or stay.

Ramla grew amazed that Abram would perform the sacrifice himself, performing the role that a priest of a particular God would take in Egypt. And the sacrifice would be not in a temple but in the open air of this meadow in Bethel. To someone else, such intimacy between God and believer might seem to be impious, but Ramla understood.

When they had arrived in Bethel a few days prior, Ramla had caught up with Eliezer and said to him, "Bethel; 'House of God'?"

"Yes," the man answered in a matter of fact manner.

"But there's no 'house' here—no temple of any kind," Ramla had thought. Then she recalled that for her—and apparently for Abram—she did not need to be in a temple to commune with the Gods.

The day wore on. She knew that Sarai would be angry that she was gone so long, but Ramla didn't care. She wanted to see what happened when Abram performed the ceremony. Near sundown, with the stone altar and wood carefully crafted, the pyre was set aflame. Then, servants led the animals to Abram. He neatly and expertly slit their jugulars so that there were no cries or pain.

One by one, the animals were laid upon the altar, and the fire consumed them, filling the whole area with the aroma of roasting meat as the smoke drifted upward towards El. Periodically, servants would feed the fire with more wood. All the while, Abram spoke words of praise to El—praise for life, for family, for promise, for health, for wealth, for everything in the world, it seemed to Ramla.

El seemed to be, for Abram, the God by Whom all things were made and given. It was as if Abram rolled the entire pantheon of Egypt's Gods into one God—El.

By the time it was dark, the last of the animals had been offered to the God. Abram took some of the last of the meat and divided it among his servants as food. This, too, amazed Ramla. Abram treated the servants as if they, too, were priests of El. There was a strong sense of collective worship that she had never witnessed. They all—master and servants—had shared in the sacrifice and then shared in the meal. Abram, with his blood-stained robe and with a grimy, smoky face, faced Ramla, held out a large, greasy portion of cooked meat, and called to her.

"Come! Take this to your mistress. Eat some for yourself."

Ramla jumped up, ran to him, and took the meat from Abram. As she turned to go, Abram's voice caused her to turn back towards him.

"Ramla," he said, loudly, "Thank you for being here. I thank El for you, as well."

The statement almost caused Ramla to burst into tears. No one had cared for her like this since Tefibi expressed his feelings so many years before back in Egypt. Abram's words rang in her ears and made Ramla smile all through Sarai's harsh scolding at being absent all day. After her mistress had eaten her fill, Ramla took a piece of the sacrifice meat and sat outside the tent.

"El, God of Abram…thank you for this meat…and thank you for my master, Abram," she prayed.

Shortly after the sacrifice days ended, Abram and Lot met in the grove near the camp. Finding some of Lot's flock among Abram's animals caused Lot's husbandmen to accuse Abram's men of theft. Everyone among Abram's group knew that the real reason was because of Lot's haphazard shepherds who cared more about drink and sleep than tending to the flock. Abram's shepherds simply took in the strays to keep them from wandering away and falling to the predators around. Eliezer made sure Abram's men were the best available, and they all held a fierce loyalty to Abram.

So, Abram asked Lot to come and clear the air between the two groups. Abram asked Lot to choose land for himself and his flocks; Abram would take the other part of the land. It was more than fair of the old man, Ramla thought. And she felt that Abram had reached his limit with the uncouth nephew. Accusing Abram's men of theft was like accusing Abram himself, she reasoned. The man was nothing if not honorable and true.

As expected by all, Lot chose what he thought was the better land, the greener pastures near the river. Sarai entertained Lot's wife, Ado, for the better part of the day of the meeting, and Ramla served them both. Ado, whose voice matched her small size, giggled when she spoke of the wealth she and her husband had accumulated since they had left Haran. She largely ignored Ramla's service of dates and watered-down wine, and instead droned on and on about the latest gossip among her servants. The only time she mentioned Ramla was to say, "Sarai, you seem to make do with only this one servant. Surely she's not enough to meet your needs."

This prompted Sarai to sniff, "She's not even competent in the least, but I make do," a remark which caused Ado to giggle again. Ramla held her tongue and simply poured more wine for the women.

The women chatted on, and soon Abram entered the tent to tell Ado that Lot was leaving. Ado embraced the air around Sarai as she stood to leave. She giggled as she passed Abram. Ramla had no time to leave the tent, so she heard Abram say, when Ado had left, "Lot is moving his flock and his tents eastward towards the river. He thinks he will settle in one of the towns there, maybe Sodom. We are moving ours to Mamre."

Sarai nodded. "You know how I feel about Lot; good riddance, I say," she said, and Ramla, who had never heard Sarai speak about the nephew, thought, "Well, at least we agree on that." "I don't like moving, you know that, my husband, but it is for the best. It will rid us of Lot and that one," Sarai said, motioning with a thumb towards the tent flap where Ado had departed. "I might like life in a town again, but I do enjoy Mamre," Sarai mused. "It is always so cool; I so like the forest there."

"As do I," Abram agreed, "But no towns, please. I had my fill of them in Ur. And Egypt." Then, to Ramla, he said, "Prepare my wife's things to move in the morning."

The next day, Ramla had bundled some of the tent's items together and bent down to place them in a growing pile outside so they could be added to one of the carts that carried the household items. As she straightened up, she noticed Abram walking behind his own tent nearby. His servants were also busily packing carpets, plates, cups, and other personal effects. But Abram seemed lost in his own world. He appeared to be speaking to the air.

Ramla made her way behind some of the other tents and positioned herself at the far corner of Abram's tent; she was close enough to hear Abram but not so close that he could detect her presence.

"Thank you, my God! You have reminded me of the promise. Yes, I believe that You will give me sons, that You will increase me and that I will be a blessing and not a curse. Yes, I believe You have promised the land to me. Thank you!" he prayed.

Ramla recalled the stories Eliezer had told her about how El had made great promises to Abram, and now she had heard Abram speak to El as if they had been in conversation with each other. Ramla had even asked Eliezer once why the older couple had no children or grandchildren. She surmised that perhaps they'd had children who had died somewhere along their journeys. No, Eliezer had told her. No children had been born, ever. She came to understand how much that grieved the couple, especially Abram.

Now, apparently, this God had reassured Abram that the promises were real, even though it seemed for the moment that Lot had been given the better land along the river. Ramla sneaked back to Sarai's tent quickly without being seen. Yet, she came away impressed again at the relationship between Abram and his God.

Ramla found out that Sarai was right about Mamre. The old, tall oak trees created a wonderful, calm garden beneath their canopies. Ramla felt that the entire forest was a sacred place where the Gods had been worshipped since the beginning of time. It had that kind of spiritual presence about it to her. She again watched as Abram built another altar to El and as he sacrificed again to his God. This time, Abram waved Ramla closer, but, out of respect, she held up her hands in front of her and shook her head, "No." Abram simply smiled and nodded; he seemed to understand and honor her feeling, and he returned to the sacrifice. She again offered a prayer of thanks to El when she ate her portion that Abram gave to her.

Life settled into a routine for Ramla for a time. She felt more content in her situation than she had before, largely, she felt, because of her increasing understanding of Abram's relationship with El.

The dynamic intrigued her. She even forgot to think about running away. She did, however, continue to take her walks. The cool green shadows of the oaks of Mamre calmed Ramla and revived her at the same time.

Her relationship with Sarai continued to be rancorous, but it quickly became overshadowed by the news that Lot, the nephew, had been captured in a war between some of the cities to the east. A straggler from a battle came through the camp one evening—a short, thick man with the grime of battle still on him—and he reported to all that the kings of five cities, including the one in which Lot and his clan had settled, went to war and were defeated. Lot and some of his group had been taken prisoner.

Between agonizingly long gulps of water from a skin, the short man gave details of where the prisoners had been taken. Sarai heard the commotion and ordered, "Go see what all that commotion is about." Ramla ran up to the group as the man was giving the final details. He had apparently also been captured, but he had managed to escape in the darkness after camp was made.

The news energized the encampment. Abram and Eliezer quickly conferred; it was decided that a large detachment of Abram's group would make a lightning raid on the prisoner camp. Ramla ran back to Sarai with the news. The old woman grabbed her skirt in fear. "Oh, my husband! Surely he will not go himself!" Ramla, also fearing for Abram, said, "Yes, I think he is leading the group, mistress."

At that moment, Abram strode into Sarai's tent. Ramla made to leave again, but Abram stopped her. "Stay, Ramla. I want you to hear this. My wife, Lot has been captured in a war. I am going to rescue him. Do not try to stop me." Sarai opened her mouth to protest, but Abram didn't seem to notice.

"Ramla, take care of my wife. I know you will," he said, smiling at her. Ramla bowed before him. For Abram, she would make nice with Sarai while he was gone. Abram then looked at the short sword he had strapped to his waist. He tried to move the sword around more to the front, but he couldn't quite get it where he wanted it.

Ramla leapt to assist him without thinking. She adjusted the strap for him and got the sword moved to where he desired it. He touched her hair and said, "Thank you, my child. May El bless you." It was the first time Abram had touched her. Ramla bowed low and thanked him in return. Sarai sat on her pillows with an open mouth, her fear for Abram replaced by jealousy in a flash. "Enough of this! If you must go, my husband, then go!"

Abram looked at Sarai, then at Ramla, then back to Sarai. "Farewell to you both until I return," he said calmly, and he went out to join his men.

ELEVEN

It took Abram and about 300 of his men almost two weeks to recapture Lot and several of his servants and many of his women. Sarai sighed with relief when news of Abram's success reached the camp. This time, when Abram entered the tent, Ramla immediately left; she wanted to give husband and wife time to rejoice over the return.

Ramla learned that Abram had led a perfect raid; he had divided his forces and confused the enemy with a night attack. Not only did he liberate Lot and his group, but he also managed to free almost all the captives. He and his mighty men escorted Lot's group back to Sodom, the city where Lot had settled, and he left word with the king of the city to send for help if needed. All of this he managed with no loss of life or limb to his men or to any of the captives.

Abram called for a celebratory feast and sacrifice dedicated to El. To make it accessible to everyone who wanted to attend, Abram ordered that the event would be held in the King's Valley that ran between Mamre's Oaks and the cities to the east. The event ran on for several days. Every member of the household, every servant and shepherd, came and enjoyed the feast and participated in the worship. Even Sarai managed to smile and laugh during the festivities. She gave Ramla leave to enjoy the festival and was served by a young girl for the duration of the event.

In the middle of the feast, the grateful king of Sodom came with gifts of thanksgiving for Abram including meats and fruits and cheeses. He and his household joined in the dancing and singing and feasting. He gave a moving speech in which he gave Abram credit for saving not only his life but also saving his city and removing the threat of the enemies. Ramla noted that he spoke well, and she knew that Abram deserved this credit and more. As though the saving of the captives weren't enough, Abram and his men had also recaptured much of the treasury of Sodom and almost all the lost livestock.

Lot and his wife came with the king, but they remained surprisingly and uncharacteristically reserved throughout, Ramla noticed, as if they had been chastised and sobered by the experience of having been taken captive.

Also in attendance was the king of Salem, a certain Melchizedek. He brought with him a vast array of breads, sweet and not, and some of the finest wine Ramla had ever tasted—which surprised her, given that the Great King in Egypt had some of the greatest wines in the world—and Melchizedek gave huge casks of it to Abram.

Ramla learned from various ones that this Melchizedek was a priest of El as well as being a king. "So," she thought, "El can call believers from anywhere, from any position, to His service." The importance of this man became evident when Abram called on

Eliezer to bring out the gifts he had prepared for Melchizedek. The crowd at the festival was stunned. Ramla could not believe it, either. Abram gave the king of Salem fully one-tenth of all he possessed—flocks, food, servants, all. The gesture clearly touched the king. He called the older man over to him, stood from his stool and asked Abram to bow. He then placed both hands on Abram's head. Then, he said, "Blessed be Abram, by El's hand, and blessed be El, who gave Abram this great victory." Ramla saw clearly that the gesture had moved Abram when he rose from his bow. The old man's eyes were clearly red with joy over the blessing. The throng about them cheered mightily.

The king of Sodom, not to be outdone, then rose to speak. This proved somewhat difficult as he was a rather portly fellow. While his gifts and gratitude towards Abram might have been genuine, his pride got the better of him, Ramla thought as he stood. To her, he seemed like the type of man who knew he was inferior and tried his best to prove otherwise.

"Ahem," he said, clearing his throat loudly to make sure all watched him. "I, too, have gifts. I propose that Abram take all the treasure he recovered from the raid on the captive camp—all the livestock, too. Sodom will take the servants back because we need them (this part, Ramla noticed, he spoke softer than the rest), but we want Abram to have the goods themselves." The king of Sodom spoke these words and spread his arms wide as he concluded.

A smattering of applause met this announcement, which surprised Sodom's king. He expected his generosity to be met with more acclaim. As he looked around for approval, Abram rose to his feet.

"That is truly generous, sir," he began. "But I have made a promise before my God." Ramla's eyes grew wide with awe at what

Abram said. She sensed what was coming. Abram continued. "I swore an oath that, if my effort was successful, I would take nothing from it—except what my men and I ate while we went and came back. However, I thank the king for his gesture." A buzz of approval ran through the crowd at this.

The king of Sodom sat down with a puzzled look. Why would anyone turn down treasure and animals? But Ramla understood; she realized that Abram did not want to be in any sort of debt to any man, especially this one. If he had accepted the king's offering, Abram would be beholding to the king at that point. And with such a large gift, the payback that Abram would have to provide would be more than he would wish to do.

Abram finished his refusal in his own elegant way. "Let anyone who wishes to take payment for what they did in rescuing these captives feel free to take what he thinks he deserves." True, appreciative applause from the crowd met this statement. Ramla noticed the king's face turn red with, she felt, both embarrassment and anger. "My master has made an enemy there," she said to herself. She also noticed that the king of Salem nodded in approval at Abram's statement.

The celebration ended, and Abram's group began to make its way back to the Oaks of Mamre. Ramla made sure Sarai had what she needed and saw her mounted on her animal. She said, "Mistress, I will be along shortly. I must make sure we have all our things." Sarai, tired from the long day, yawned, then told Ramla, "I am not waiting for you. But don't dawdle. Catch up as soon as you can."

When Sarai had moved out of sight, Ramla turned to search for Melchizedek. She spotted him as he was mounting his horse to depart. Abram stood next to it and held the reins as the king settled on the animal's back. Ramla, throwing protocol to the wind, ran up behind Abram and stood quietly, breathing heavily but quietly. Melchizedek noticed her and looked over Abram's head at her. Abram followed the king's eyes and turned to see Ramla.

"Ah, my king," he said smiling at Ramla. "This is my wife's servant girl, Ramla. She has been with us since we were in Egypt." At this introduction, Ramla bowed low before Melchizedek.

"Rise, my daughter," the king said. "I know of you. I dreamt of you. In my dream, I saw you running among the brown rushes along a large river. And I saw you watching all that happened today very closely. May El bless you, my child."

Ramla allowed herself a small smile. The king's dream was meant as a sign to her that he was one who was in touch with the Gods. She gracefully stood and felt that it would be permitted to look up at the king on the tall horse. When she did, she saw his smile and his hand raised in blessing for her. Abram, too, wore a smile. He handed the leather reins to Melchizedek, and the king turned his animal towards Salem.

With this, Abram turned back to Ramla and said, "So! You have been blessed by the High Priest of El. What do you think of that, eh?"

Ramla bowed her head in reverence. "I…I think I want to know more of this God Who blesses me."

"Perhaps you can," Abram smiled at her, and together they moved towards their own waiting animals.

TWELVE

A bram took Melchizedek's blessing of Ramla as a sign for him to begin talking directly to Ramla about El. "Unseemly!" Sarai said in the presence of both Abram and Ramla when he told her about his plans. Abram understood his wife's jealousy, but this did not stop him from speaking to the young woman about the God. He reassured Sarai that his instruction with Ramla would not interfere with her duties in Sarai's tent, and finally Sarai sighed and nodded.

The discussions about El that began between the old man and the young servant woman caused some servants to gossip. Abram knew better than to speak to Ramla in his wife's tent. So, the pair would walk in the forest and sometimes stay by a watering hole or well and speak. Ramla, not wanting to pry too much into her master's personal relationship with Sarai, still was curious as to what Sarai thought about El. It took her some weeks to muster the courage to ask, "If I may be bold, sir, what did my mistress think of your directions from El?"

The old man licked his lips, and his eyes smiled. "Ah, I wondered when you would ask about my wife and El. It is a fair question.

Abram asked Ramla during those talks about her life before meeting them. Ramla told him what she remembered and how she had been promised to the Goddess and how she had told the priest at the temple on the Nile that Gods do not need to be in temples to be seen and worshipped.

"And now, you understand that what you said as a child has come true for you," Abram said as they walked in the forest together. Abram stopped and used his walking stick to poke at an animal's hole in the ground, and that gave Ramla a moment to say, "Yes, but I think the Goddess speaks to me that way as well."

Abram silently considered this possibility as well as he probed the ground. "Perhaps," he said straightening up and continuing to stroll. "Or perhaps it was El masquerading as your Goddess all along."

Ramla didn't understand the word. "Can you say that again?" she asked, adding, "I'm sorry for my lack of language."

"It's fine," he said. "I mean that your Goddess speaking to you was not the Goddess, but it was El," Abram explained.

"Ah, I see what you are saying," she said. Now it was Ramla's turn to ponder this possibility. The thought intrigued her.

"When El speaks to you, do you hear a voice or do you have a feeling inside you?" she asked Abram.

He smiled and reminded her of how El first came to him while Abram shepherded in Haran. "It is a definitely a voice. Clear. Calm. But with power behind it. It is interesting, though; the voice is masculine, but it sounds young."

"Y…young?" Ramla asked, holding a tree branch back so that they could walk without it hitting them.

"Yes, a young man's voice. And you? The Goddess? A voice or…"

"No, not a voice," Ramla said with a touch of sadness in her tone. "Words, yes. Words, but in my heart and head. The Goddess speaks to me inside me," she explained. She looked at Abram sideways to see his reaction as they walked on. He seemed to nod in understanding. What she wanted to tell him was that she was jealous that El spoke to him directly, while her Goddess only put words in her heart.

Abram seemed to sense Ramla's sadness in the quiet that followed. He tried to make her feel better. "I have gone for some months without El speaking to me. It must be wonderful to have the God speak to your heart directly," he said.

Ramla smiled at this. She knew Abram said it to make her feel better, but perhaps he was right. "I need to think about what you said—that the Goddess and El are one and the same."

Abram held his hand out and stopped Ramla. Turning to her, he said, with a touch of tenderness to his voice, "That's not what I meant, exactly. I meant that perhaps El was using your Goddess to speak to you. Maybe it was El's voice in the Goddess's messages to you all these years."

"Ah, I understand now," she said, looking up at Abram. The kindness in his eyes captivated her. Not having memories of her father, she now thought of this man as the closest thing to a father she would ever have.

"We need to return," he said. "Your mistress will worry about both of us."

They smiled at each other and walked on in silence.

The next morning, Ramla was awake and preparing the meal for the sleeping Sarai when Abram entered the tent. His wide eyes seemed to Ramla to be almost boyish with excitement. "El spoke to me before dawn!" he said, barely able to contain himself.

The words caused Sarai to stir. "What is it, my husband," she said, sitting up with a yawn. "Is there trouble?"

Ramla dried her hands on a cloth and came towards Abram with her own wide eyes. "What did El say?" Ramla asked, forgetting for the moment that Sarai was there. This exclamation jolted Sarai into complete wakefulness.

"Watch your tone!" she said to Ramla sharply. "Who are you to demand anything of my husband?" Ramla quickly bowed her head, stepped back from Abram and returned to her work. "That one is becoming too familiar with you," Sarai said, jerking a thumb at Ramla. "I knew bad things would come of you two being together."

"Dear wife," Abram said, patiently, "I came to tell you that El spoke to me again in a dream."

"Oh, no!" Sarai exclaimed. "Surely we are not moving again!"

"No, no," Abram calmed her, showing her both hands. "This is good news. El renewed the promise!" he said, the excitement returning to his voice.

Again, Sarai yawned and said, "So, El said nothing new." Then, to Ramla, she demanded, "Where's my water, girl?" But Ramla had stopped her chores when Abram had spoken. She knelt, open mouthed, waiting for Abram to finish what he was saying. Sarai's lack of interest in El's message and Ramla's obvious interest struck Abram. It hurt him when Sarai didn't seem to care about his conversations with El.

It was Abram who brought Ramla back to the present. "Do as your mistress says, Ramla. I will speak to you later. I bid you good day, my wife," he said shortly, and turned and left.

Sarai's voice followed him. "Yes! Speak to her later. As you always do!" And then, to Ramla, she said, "And you! Get back to work. And bring me my water!"

Ramla could hardly wait until she found time later in the day so she could seek out Abram. She found him with Eliezer, looking at some sheep in an enclosure not far from the camp. She waited at a respectful distance until the men finished their business before approaching Abram.

"My master, would you have a moment to tell me what El told you in your dream?" Abram smiled at her and then turned back to the animal pen.

"Yes, of course. I was only now speaking to Eliezer about some animals for a sacrifice that El asked of me," Abram explained. He turned from the pen and took his staff that leaned on the enclosure and headed to see another group of animals in the adjoining field. Ramla followed at his side as he told her of the dream.

"As I said this morning, El renewed the promises—in fact, all of them: That I will have a son and that I will possess the land El will give me," he said, the excitement of the morning still in his voice. "El promised protection as well; as a shield around me, so would El's protection be."

Ramla dared to interrupt him. "Was it the same voice you have heard before?" she asked.

"Yes," Abram said, her question not interrupting his story or rhythm. They moved quickly through the small copse of trees that led to the next meadow as Abram continued. "I voiced my concern that Eliezer—a good and capable man, Ramla—would be my heir at this point if something happened to me."

"I know he is good, sir. He has always been kind with me," she added.

"I know, even if he is short sometimes." Abram continued as they walked on. "So, El said that no, Eliezer would not be my heir, that my son would be—the son El would give me."

Ramla interrupted again, her excitement for Abram uncontained. "Master! That is wonderful. I am so happy..." she said, "for you."

"And there is more, my child," he said to Ramla patiently. "In the dream, El took me out of the tent and into the night outside the camp. He told me to look into the heavens and to count the stars. Of course, there were too many to number," he said, with a small chuckle of enthusiasm. "El promised that my sons and daughters will be as this."

Abram slowed a bit as they entered the meadow. The sudden burst of sun after being in the trees caused both of them to pause and shield their eyes for a moment before continuing towards the animals. A shepherd nearby waved in greeting as Ramla said, "Wonderful, master! Wonderful!"

"Yes, and..." Abram paused, looking about him and deciding which group of animals to inspect in the field before moving that way. "Then El spoke at length of possessing the land of promise. I asked El how I would know this to be true."

"You...you questioned the God?" Ramla asked incredulously.

"Mmmm," Abram said in acknowledgement. "But don't misunderstand me, Ramla; I believe in El. I believe in the promises." He turned to her, and she sensed that Abram was making an important point about this. She looked at him, and Abram said, "Do you understand? I believe in El."

Ramla nodded. She understood that his belief was not only a simple belief that the God existed. Abram also trusted the promises and planned his life around them. That, she reasoned, was what real belief must be.

Abram scoured the large flock of sheep and seemed to be looking for something in particular. "And now, El is asking for a sacrifice to show that the promise of the land will be fulfilled. El has asked for a heifer, a goat, a ram, and two birds to be offered. We are here to find some suitable animals to offer."

"Oh, I see," Ramla said, concentrating on the animals for the first time. She knew that the Gods liked only the best animals, the ones without blemish or spot or disease. No old or weak animals for the Gods. She knew that one never offered something common to the Gods.

Abram spoke with the shepherds and told them what was required. For much of the afternoon, Ramla trailed behind Abram as he worked his way through his flocks, speaking to this man or that one, finding what El required. Finally, as the sun drew low on the horizon, Abram felt satisfied that the appropriate animals had been set aside for the sacrifice. "Tomorrow afternoon, we will sacrifice to El," he said to Ramla as she was saying her farewell to return to Sarai's tent.

"We?" Ramla said, noting that Abram seemed to emphasize the word.

"Yes, of course. I wish for you to be there, as always, my child. If you wish it for yourself."

"Yes, please, sir!" Ramla said with pride and excitement.

Early the next day, as was the custom, Abram and his men began to construct a new, bigger altar from carefully selected stones that had been brought from the river with sledges pulled by animals. The wood, too, had been cut to the same lengths and neatly stacked to the side of the growing stone structure, ready for use that afternoon.

Ramla could not escape her duties that day to watch the building; it was laundry day, and she took extra time to clean Sarai's bedclothes and cloths with care in the large cooking pots so that no fault would be found in them. Having prepared the evening meal in advance, making sure all the clean items were stored and in their proper places, and asking permission, Ramla was granted time by Sarai to watch the sacrifice.

"I suppose you may go," Sarai sniffed with resignation. "You will probably run away to watch it in any case. At least you asked my leave this time."

Ramla ran to reach the sacrifice meadow, a bit disappointed that she did not see the altar being put together. Before she reached the clearing, she noticed with curiosity that the smoke from the pyre wasn't rising over the site; that meant that the fire had not been lit. When she finally ran into the clearing, she spied no servants or any of Abram's hired men. All that was there was the completed altar and the animals—but the animals had been cut exactly in half. The air hung thick around the meadow with the blood and the buzzing of flies on the exposed flesh and entrails.

Then Ramla saw the birds. Abram, waving his staff in both hands, was between the halves of the animals, shooing away several large buzzards as they flapped closer and closer to the carcasses.

"Ramla!" Abram called when he spied her, "come! Help me!"

Ramla sprinted towards Abram, instantly understanding what he meant. She spread her arms wide and yelled, "Yaaaaaaah!" The large, white-winged birds took flight at the screaming, running young woman. Abram joined her in her cry, and together they kept the hungry birds away.

"Sir, what is happening?" Ramla asked between attacks by the buzzards. "Why are the animals like this and not on the altar?"

"El's request," Abram answered. "El asked that I cut the animals in two and spread them apart. All except the small birds." Ramla then took notice of the small lattice box that contained the two birds El had asked for. Until the sun set, the pair fought to keep the carrion eaters away from El's animals, taking a moment for water when the birds moved farther away. As the last of the sun's rays left, Abram said wearily, "Good! The birds will stay gone now that darkness is coming."

Abram then walked over to where the altar had been built and reached down into a shallow pit where long, thin pieces of wood lay smoldering from the bundle of burning coals prepared for the altar's fire. He pulled out one such piece and lit two oil-soaked torches nearby. In the torchlight, Ramla noticed that Abram looked tired, his normally smooth face looking much older than usual.

"I…I think we must wait for El to instruct us," he said wearily. "I will lie down for a moment. Ramla, would you please stay awake for me? Please do not hesitate to wake me if you need me."

The young woman understood. As Abram spread out a thick woolen blanket to lie down on, Ramla sat cross-legged at Abram's feet and faced the halved animals. In the flickering of the torch lights, the half carcasses cast eerie shadows on the grass beyond. Normally, Ramla feared little, but there was something mysterious and unsettling about El's request. Now, to have to sit alone while Abram slept—all of it felt strange to her.

Abram quickly fell asleep. Ramla shifted and pulled her knees up to her chin as she sat, wrapping her arms round her legs. The wind picked up, making the torches dance even more wildly and giving a murmuring, haunted song to the forest beyond the clearing. Despite the season and the wind being somewhat warm, Ramla shivered involuntarily. She looked up to the wide belt of stars above her. "El, God of Abram, if you are there, answer this good man's prayer; give him children, and give him wisdom. Please," she prayed silently.

As if in answer, Abram's sleep became troubled. He spoke mumbling words and thrashed about. Ramla couldn't understand much of what he said, but she clearly saw his dreaming caused him grief. She debated about waking him, but she also knew well that one of the God's most common ways of speaking to people was through sleep. So, despite being conflicted by Abram's writhing and muffled cries, she sat silent and still.

Suddenly, Abram awoke and sat up with a start with a large gasp for air. The young woman jumped back with alarm. Abram looked about him, wide-eyed and breathing heavily. Ramla, her senses returned from the fright, stood and said, "Master! It is I—Ramla. All is well." She bent down and grabbed a skin of water. "Here, sir. You were having a bad dream. I watched it for some time."

Abram blinkingly looked up into her face. Still gasping, he took the skin and swigged the water, much of it landing on his beard and chest. He handed the skin back to her and said, "Yes…yes, a dream. From El. And a message."

Ramla waited patiently until Abram continued. "El said again that my offspring would be too numerous to mention. But then, he told me about great catastrophe awaiting my children. For many generations, they would be slaves in another country—but then, El would free them and prosper them. I, he said, would live a long life and return to the earth peacefully." The old man's eyes glistened with tears as he spoke.

"But I have no children," he said, continuing to cry. "Why is El not providing?"

At that moment, Ramla looked beyond Abram; her eyes grew wide with amazement. "Master, look!" she exclaimed. Abram turned on his blanket, and then he, too, leapt to his feet. A torch that looked like a pillar of fire, taller than a man, began moving slowly on the path between the two animals. Behind it, a large, dark clay pot, smoke billowing over its sides like a caldron, filled the clearing with sweet-smelling vapors. The pair stared at the fire and the smoke. Abram, without taking his eyes off the phenomenon, said softly to Ramla, "Do you see…this?"

Filled with awe and wonder, Ramla could not answer; she only nodded slowly. Abram didn't question her further. The fire and smoke traveled back and forth between the length of the carcasses, consuming the flesh in a much shorter time than if Abram would have sacrificed it himself. After the animals had been burned, the fire and smoke disappeared as quickly as they came. All that Abram and Ramla saw was the charred ground where the animals had been in the flickering torchlight. Suddenly, the wind that had been whipping all night ceased. It was as if all the air had been sucked out of the meadow.

The pair looked at each other, open-mouthed and wide-eyed. Abram said, "Did you hear the promise?"

"He…hear? Hear the promise? No, sir. I heard nothing," Ramla said. "What promise?"

"El," Abram said excitedly, "El told me that my people, my children and my children's children, would have the land from the Nile to the Euphrates—all of it! El consuming the sacrifice with His own fire was the sign that this was true. Truly, El provides all!"

Ramla considered before answering. She wanted to be honest with Abram. "I heard nothing, my lord," she said with a bit of sadness in her voice.

"Yes…yes," Abram replied, looking up at the burned ground in front of them. "El provides." The first glimmers of daylight began to paint the sky with a soft yellow glow through the woods behind them. The pair spoke little, each consumed with thoughts as they began to gather their belongings and head back to camp. It was Ramla who spoke as they left the clearing.

"Sir," she began, "what we saw; it was as if El had made a contract with you and sealed it with the sacrifice."

Abram smiled broadly. "My child, I was thinking the same thing." She returned his smile and, together, they made their way home.

THIRTEEN

For several years, Ramla continued to serve Sarai. Many times, the contentious nature of her mistress caused Ramla to seriously consider running away. But her admiration for Abram, along with her increasing interest in Abram's God, kept her in Sarai's tent at those times. Her pride in doing a good job for her mistress, even when stressed by her, kept Ramla there the rest of the time.

Abram and Sarai argued often about their inability to have children. When Sarai broached the subject, Abram recalled, it was usually because someone had made a remark to her about children or she had seen a particularly happy child running or skipping around the camp. This time, however, Sarai vented her anger at El.

"Your God! Your God seems powerless to deliver on the promises made to you. 'You will be the father of many nations!'" she said mockingly. "Ha! This is not going to happen with me. You need to realize that," she told Abram. She laughed about El's covenant ceremony, recalling that the "covenant" seemed to be between El and him and Ramla. Abram could hear the bitterness in her voice as she spoke.

"Take that…that Hagar. Have a child with her. You two seem as thick as thieves anyway. You don't think I've not heard the gossip? The whole camp thinks you have bedded her already."

"Oh, my dear one, how can you say that? I know you're angry and frustrated, but you know that is not true," Abram said sadly. Abram had not included Sarai in the ceremony simply because he knew she remained skeptical about El's promises. But now, he saw how hurt his wife was, how sad his princess was, because of not being able to provide an heir for him. He remembered the look of sadness in her eyes when other servants carried their children with them as they went about their chores. His love for her, despite her sometimes-difficult disposition, still burned strong and deep.

"I…I'm sorry, my husband," Sarai said, realizing that she had perhaps crossed a line because of the look of anguish on Abram's face. She hung her head.

"Her pride was wounded so deeply," Abram thought, as he watched his wife's cheeks run with tears. But for some reason this time felt different to him; there was a bitterness and jealousy to it. He knelt to her cushions and touched her cheek affectionately. Sarai turned her head into his hand and kissed it, her tears washing his fingers and palm.

"You know I cannot take Ramla, my dear one," Abram said, as Sarai continued to cry and kiss his hand. "I…I care about her like a daughter."

"Oh, you can," Sarai laughed bitterly, her jealousy replacing her hurt for the moment as she pulled away from Abram's hand. "Take her. I promise that I will raise the child as our own."

Abram sat back on the cushions to take a better look at Sarai to see if she were being sarcastic or serious. She knew his look. "I am serious," she said, answering his unasked question. Then, knowing where to strike Abram, she added, "Besides, El's promise did not say that your heir would have to come from me, did it?"

Abram had not considered that possibility. He turned his head in thought. "No," he agreed, "the promise never specified. You are right, my dear."

Sarai sniffed and dried her cheeks with her sleeve. She was again hurt, but this time her pain came from how quickly Abram agreed with her to take another woman. Yet, Sarai resolved to not let him know how deeply she was wounded. No, she thought, she would take her revenge out on Hagar.

"Then it's settled," she said, her composure hastened by her jealousy. "I will tell her to expect you tonight. Come here. All will be ready. The child of the promise will come from her, but we will raise the child as our own."

"If you truly desire it, my wife," Abram said, standing. He, too, felt a twinge of sadness that Sarai would so easily share him with another woman.

"Yes, I desire it," Sarai lied.

She waited until Abram left before bursting into tears again.

"No, mistress," Ramla pleaded, her dark eyes wide with fear and surprise, when Sarai told her what was required. "Please. I beg of you, do not do this thing." For Ramla, she thought she could not sink any lower in life. Now, to be forced into the bed of this man, even if she respected him as she did—especially because she respected him so much. She thought of her promises before the Goddess. She thought of her mother who dedicated her at an early age. She thought of her own pride which told her that such a thing was not only beneath her, but it was also unworthy of the Gods.

But Sarai turned a deaf ear to her protestations. She even wore a perverse and wry smile as she again ordered the younger woman to make herself ready to receive Abram.

"You will do it because I said you will," Sarai said with finality. "It is no use arguing about it. You have no say in the matter. When will you learn that you must do as you are told?"

"But mistress, please!" Ramla said, begging and beginning to cry. "I...I...I,"

"What?" Sarai demanded. "Spit it out, girl."

Ramla struggled to say it, "I have never been with a man before."

Sarai's eyes brightened. Her slight self-satisfied smile grew a little wider. "I should hope not," she said. "Do you think I would give you to my husband if you had been soiled or tainted by someone else?"

Ramla sobbed and sank to her knees, and then over onto one side on the tent floor. Sarai stood above her, still smiling that same, almost evil smile. She seemed to revel in the younger woman's misery.

Sarai's face grew hard and said, "You seem to enjoy spending time with my husband. Now here's your chance to spend even more. So, dry your eyes, wash your face, and put on something decent. My husband will be here this evening. You will do whatever he asks you to do because it is your place to obey." Sarai smiled one more time at Ramla then left her alone.

Ramla's lips said, "Yes, mistress," as Sarai left, but her heart burned with resentment and anger towards the older woman. Was she being punished for talking to Abram about El? Was Sarai so petty and jealous and spiteful that she would hurt her this way?

"What kind of God would allow this to happen?" Ramla thought bitterly through her tears because of the great indignity and insult to her person that would befall her that night.

It was not that Abram had ever been rude to her or insulted her in any manner; he had not. No, the opposite was true. He had at times gone out of his way to be kind to her and show concern for her needs. He even seemed to realize how much of a crone his beloved Sarah could be. She knew that in Abram she had a common bond of being able to communicate with the Gods.

She could run away. Now. It was finally time. While Sarai busied herself elsewhere.

Her cheeks still glistening with tears, Ramla looked outside the tent flap that faced away from the compound to see who might be looking that way. A young man with a sword, one of Eliezer's men who had made the raid on the captive group, stood on the left of the opening. He said, "Can I help you, miss?" when Ramla looked his way.

"No...no. Thank you," she answered. Ramla ran to the front of the tent and looked there as well. Sticking her head out, she saw that another one of Eliezer's armed men also stood there. He only turned and nodded to Ramla when she looked out. Ramla closed the tent flap slowly.

It began to dawn on Ramla that she was trapped.

She considered her options. She could do herself harm, but part of her pride, the inborn part that reminded her of her mother, forbade it. She thought of talking to the Goddess or to El, but she felt completely abandoned by all Gods at that point. All she could think of was to try to talk Abram out of hurting her when he came. At least, she thought, she would not obey Sarai's order to prepare herself. She wanted to Abram to see her grief-streaked face and her sorrow.

All too soon, Abram appeared in the tent. He found Ramla slumped in her corner, crying softly. He stood at the front and said, "My child. How do you feel? Are you unwell?"

Ramla's confusion showed in her face. "I...do not want to do this. I thought you cared for me. Why are you doing this?" she asked Abram, looking up through her tears.

"Come here, please," he said. She stayed in her corner, so Abram repeated, "Come. I won't hurt you. I promise." With a sob, Ramla slowly rose and walked to Abram. She stood before him with her head on her chest.

He reached down to her and gently wiped a tear from her face. "I know you're miserable here, Ramla," Abram said soothingly. He, too, seemed to show sadness. "Believe me, this is not my choice. I would never purposely hurt you. My wife insists on this. It was not my idea."

"And you must obey her?" Ramla asked, her eyes still downcast. All sense of protocol left her. "Are you her slave, too?"

Abram pondered this last question. "Yes, in a sense, I am. She is still and will always be my wife. I would give her anything she asked of me, within reason." This answer only made Ramla's crying louder, her slender shoulders trembling with each sniffle. Abram suddenly realized how much fear lay behind Ramla's emotions.

"You...you said, 'Within reason'? Where...where is the reason in this?" she asked. Again, Abram considered.

"All I can offer you is this: El has promised children to me." Now it was Abram's turn to show his emotions. His own eyes began to be wet with tears. "I…I cannot tell you how much my heart aches for a child, a son, to be my heir and to dedicate him to El." Abram's words and his sincere tears caused Ramla to feel a twinge of sadness for the old man. Her own tears subsided, and she looked up at Abram with concern and care.

"My master," she said slowly, choosing her words carefully, "I am saddened that this is happening. You must know that."

"I do," he whispered. "I know this is asking more of you than one should." Through his tears, he added, "I will not do this thing if you do not wish it."

Ramla could not believe her ears. "Really?" she said, incredulously. "Oh, my master, thank you! No one has given me a choice in my life since I can remember. Yes, but I am also saddened that El has not yet given you a son. I see your brokenness before El."

Then, realizing what that meant to them both, Ramla asked, "What will we tell your wife?"

Abram thought of this, his own tears drying as well. "I don't know, my child. Let us sleep tonight. In the morning, we will decide what to tell her."

The pair laughed slightly, which was a welcome break of the tension and sadness in the tent. "Thank you, sir," Ramla said, becoming serious again for a moment.

Abram stretched and sat on Sarai's bed cushions. Ramla returned to her corner. "Are you ready for bed?" Abram asked her. "Yes, my master," she answered. He doused the bright, wide oil lamp that hung in the middle of the tent and, soon, both of them slept, worn out from the emotions of the evening.

Ramla dreamed. A younger man sat on a rock near the camp, and she approached him. She asked if he needed anything. She sensed that he was a messenger of some kind. He didn't answer her question; he simply smiled at her and said, "You know that El will bless you. Abram has great regard for you."

Ramla awoke from the dream with a start. It was still dark outside. Abram, unlike his wife, snored softly. She blinked her eyes wider and thought for a moment. She realized that her care for Abram and her gratitude towards his kindness meant more to her than almost anything in her life.

Rising silently, she moved towards Abram's sleeping form. In the darkness, she gently shook him. He raised up, took her by the hand, and helped her down to the bed with him. With his other hand, he covered her with the blanket.

FOURTEEN

Sarai received the news of Ramla's pregnancy with stony silence. For her part, Ramla tried to continue as before; she still served her mistress as best she could, providing for every need Sarai had. Ramla wanted to make sure that the older woman would have no reason to complain about her service; she would force Sarai to have to invent something to complain about to Abram.

After a few weeks, Ramla's stomach settled from the nauseating feelings in the morning and started to show a slight roundness to it. Her sleep grew more and more restless, and she had less energy to perform her daily tasks, but this made her redouble her efforts to meet Sarai's needs. Such was her pride.

Abram, who showered her with tearful gratitude immediately after their union, continued to treat her with great respect. He made it a point to greet her when he entered the tent, even if his greeting angered his wife. Abram praised El for the great gift of the child; he said he knew it to be a son. Ramla, out of the hearing of Sarai, agreed with him.

She noticed, too, that Eliezer treated her with more kindness, even though the child inside her, were it to be a male, would supplant him as Abram's heir. Eliezer began to stop by occasionally to see if Ramla needed anything or simply to say hello. His usual terseness remained, but Ramla could tell a difference in his demeanor towards her. She thought a lesser man might show jealousy. His actions only served to remind Ramla that Abram had chosen well when he hired Eliezer to be his second in command.

Then, one midday, as Ramla bent to place a tray of sweet meats before Sarai for the meal, a sharp pain seemed to stab her in the side. Ramla reacted by jerking up suddenly with a loud cry, the tray of food being turned upside down on top of Sarai.

This proved to be Sarai's breaking point. She screamed at Ramla, "You fool! How dare you! You did this on purpose! You think you're better than me. You think you're better than all of us!" The sight of the food on Sarai's hair and face and clothes, coupled with the rantings she now rained down on Ramla's ears, proved too much for the younger woman. Ramla began to smile, and then, uncontrollably, to laugh and laugh at Sarai.

This threw Sarai for a moment, and her rantings stopped. She could not believe that Ramla would laugh in her face. The decade of abuse she had heaped upon Ramla now came flooding out of the younger woman, but Sarai felt as if Ramla laughed at her for not being able to have children. The moment of absurdity in Ramla's mind caused Sarai to now scream threats and abuses at Ramla even more loudly. This, in turn, made Ramla laugh even more.

The noise of the scene carried across the compound of the camp. Servants and the women of the herdsmen and their children came out of their tents to hear the yelling and the uproarious laughter coming from Sarai's tent. Abram, who had been out in the fields, came into the large circle of tents at that moment and, noticing the entire camp standing outside and listening, asked, "What is everyone doing? Why aren't you working?"

No one wanted to say. They looked at each other as the noise continued. Abram could hear the yelling and laughter, but it took a servant woman's boy of about seven years to bring the answer clearly to him. "Sir, we are listening to the fight coming from mistress Sarai's tent."

Abram's face grew dark. "Everyone!" he yelled, uncharacteristically. "Get back to your chores and homes. At once!" he ordered. The women and children scampered back inside their shelters, but they peeked out to see Abram stride purposefully towards his wife's tent.

The scene that lay before him as he entered Sarai's tent confused Abram. His wife sat on her cushions, her hair and clothes covered with food. Sarai was screaming threats and curses at Ramla, who lay nearby, rolling in loud laughter on one of the tent's carpets. Abram took in the ridiculous scene for a moment, shocked into inaction. He came to his senses and commanded, loudly, "Enough! Stop this, at once!"

Sarai and Ramla obeyed; Sarai stopped mid-threat, her index finger pointed accusatorily at the young woman, and Ramla sat up quickly and silently. "What happened here?" he asked, more to himself than the women. Sarai saw her opportunity and resumed her tirade.

"This one! This...Hagar! She threw the food on me on purpose!" Sarai claimed. "Then, she laughed at me. My husband, this woman has always thought that she was my better. Now that she is with child, she thinks it even more."

Abram considered Sarai's accusation and looked at Ramla. The Egyptian, now completely serious, looked at Abram and shook her head slowly. "You deny this, Ramla?"

Ramla quickly thought of her options. If she contradicted Sarai, the fight would escalate. If she confessed to something she didn't do, she would be lying to Abram and before the Gods. She stopped shaking her head and simply bowed before Abram.

"See? I told you. She doesn't deny it," Sarai said with triumph in her voice. It surprised Sarai that Ramla wouldn't defend herself from the blatant lie. Sarai knew that dropping the tray of food on her could only have been an accident. In a small way, Ramla's humility made Sarai hate her even more, and her eyes narrowed at the younger woman. "What is her game?" Sarai thought.

But it was Abram who studied Ramla even more closely. The action that Sarai accused her of went against everything that Abram knew of the young woman. Even the laughter seemed out of character for her. Despite her refusal to audibly deny Sarai's accusation, Abram knew in his heart that Ramla could not have done what his wife said she did. He paused a moment and hoped that Ramla would answer somehow.

Now Abram found himself in a bind. He couldn't very well call his wife a liar, especially in front of her servant. On the other hand, he felt strongly that Ramla was innocent. Ramla's silence on the matter made his choice for him.

For her part, as Ramla looked up and searched Abram's face, she confessed to her own heart that she harbored feelings of superiority to Sarai. After all, the Gods had blessed her, not Sarai, with the bearing of Abram's child. If Sarai had found any favor at all, surely Abram's El would have given her children. So, she knew that Sarai's accusations held some truth to them. That guilt added to her silence.

In that moment, Sarai's anger and jealousy towards Ramla found voice—directed at Abram. "You!" she said, using the same tone to her husband that she used with her servant, "This is on you as well. I gave her to you so that we could have the child we both wanted. I trusted you in this. And..." Sarai's voice cracked and softened into a sob of her broken heart, "and you loved her. And now," she continued, her voice finding it's anger again, "and now, she feels so superior."

At this, Abram looked at Ramla with raised eyebrows. He had not considered that Ramla might feel this way. And for her part, Ramla could not hide her contempt for Sarai before Abram. He asked her calmly, "So, do you? Do you feel superior to your mistress, Ramla?"

Ramla pulled at her fingers and bit her lower lip. She could not lie. "Yes, sir," she said softly.

"There! She...admits it!" Sarai exclaimed, her voice betraying a bit of surprise at Ramla's admission.

"But this is not my doing," Abram cried, turning on Sarai. He felt frustrated with his wife for blaming him. "All of this was your idea. You insisted that you should give her to me. You said the child would be ours. No, my wife," he said, his voice softening a bit, "you were the one who suggested this," he added, looking back at Ramla as she began to cry softly. He came back to Sarai. "Clean yourself from the food," he ordered. Without looking at her, he added "Ramla, help her."

"And do what you want with her," he said, nodding his head towards Ramla. "She is your servant, after all," he said as he turned to go. His anger at Sarai for blaming him for the issue blinded him to the consequences his words would have for Ramla.

Yet, his thoughts turned towards the Egyptian woman as he walked away. It confused Abram that Ramla felt the superior way she did towards Sarai. Perhaps it made sense, he finally reasoned. He considered that she must have felt that way, coming as she did from Pharaoh's household to live in tents; and serving his difficult wife might cause anyone to feel resentment. He felt some shame that he had never thought of this before.

"Mistress," Ramla began a moment after Abram left the tent, "I humbly apolo…"

Sarai cut her off. "Shut. Up," she ordered in a slow, reasoned voice.

Ramla's face showed fear as the older woman slowly stood and moved to where she stood over her. The younger woman held her hands up in supplication. "But my mistress, I…" Ramla started again.

"Did you not hear me?" Sarai said in a voice that was both calm and frightening at the same time. "I. Said. Shut. Up."

The anger in her eyes scared Ramla. In all the tantrums and scoldings and yellings, Ramla never before witnessed so much pain and anger so plainly etched on the older woman's face. In that moment, Ramla recalled the faces of mad men and women she had seen in Egypt. Sarai wore that sort of look now.

The sweetmeats dropped off Sarai's shoulders and hair onto Ramla and on the carpet. Sarai's anger at all of it—the pregnancy, the feelings her beloved husband felt towards Ramla, the relationship the servant girl shared with Abram concerning El, and Ramla's innate lack of treachery as well as youth and looks—came pouring out of Sarai at that moment.

Ramla's hands of supplication became coverings as Sarai began raining blows on her head and face with her fists.

FIFTEEN

The sky showed no traces of dawn the next morning when Ramla silently rose from her space near the opening of her small tent, grabbed a skin of water and a few things in a bundle, and slipped out of the camp. She knew which direction to go; she had always oriented her day around the direction of her homeland.

She knew the bruises on her face were there despite the fact that they were covered somewhat by her brown skin. She didn't remember the words Sarai used when beating her, but she would remember the feeling for the rest of her life. She vowed to never suffer such a beating again.

The internal wounds hurt her, too. It deeply saddened her that Abram would care about her so little as to turn her over to Sarai to "do what you want with her." She felt betrayed, even, because she felt that she and Abram shared much more than a bed that night.

By the time the sun rose on her, Ramla had put good distance between her and Abram's encampment at the Oaks of Mamre. She knew enough to travel quickly while it was cool, and she stopped often to rest under small shade trees during the heat of the day. She did not let a well or stream go by that she did not refill her water skin.

Twice that first day, she saw groups of travelers at a distance, and her heart leapt into her throat, thinking that they had come after her. But no. It seemed that she had not been followed.

Once she felt safe that the other travelers she saw had no connection to Abram's group, she became brave enough to ask them about both sources of water and her route. She knew to keep the morning sun on her left and the evening sun on her right.

In a land filled with caravans, traders, and nomads, almost no one thought this young, pregnant woman was traveling by herself. Most assumed she had been separated from her group. The only thing she had to worry about was to make sure that none of the caravans were slave traders or worse.

It took Ramla only a few short days of this routine of traveling very early in the day and in the cool of the evening to reach the edge of the desert. She knew that the worst of her journey lay ahead of her. Thoughts of Egypt and home—and not wanting to be in the presence of Sarai—pushed her on when she grew tired.

Back in camp, Sarai realized quite early the first day that Ramla had made her escape from the encampment. She initially felt satisfaction at the thought. The missing morning water jug at the bedside and the absence of Ramla's quiet preparation of Sarai's morning meal and necessities caused the older woman to nod her head with understanding. Sarai felt no little satisfaction at having run her younger rival away. She waited until late in the morning to inform Abram, and that waiting did not go unnoticed by Abram.

"When did you notice that she left my wife?" Abram asked when he heard that Ramla was missing. Sarai hesitated, realizing that she may have tipped her hand to her husband. "I knew she was gone earlier," Sarai said, defensively, "but I thought she might have simply wondered off somewhere. I warned you about how she can be."

"You beat her?" Abram asked, but Sarai knew what her husband said was not a question rather than an accusation.

"And why not?" Sarai sneered. "You told me to do what I wanted with her." She felt a stab of jealousy as she saw Abram realize his words the previous day caused Ramla to suffer the thrashing she received at Sarai's hand. The wound inside her pressed her to continue. "You can't know what it was like, every day, having her hold it over my head that she thought her filth didn't stink."

"Especially after," Sarai added with a pause, the hurt of her inability to conceive for her husband still stinging, "after she had been with you; she herself told you she has been prideful and petty."

Abram thought for a moment. "I never heard her say that, exactly," he corrected. "So, if she has been gone for some hours, it is unlikely we will be able to find her," he said with sadness in his voice. More than the fact that Hagar carried his child, Abram's affection for the young woman was genuine. "Besides, she carries with her my child, the promise of El to us. Or have you forgotten, my wife? And have you forgotten your promises concerning that child?" Abram asked.

Sarai narrowed her eyes at Abram. "You always say that El will provide. Well, believe it now again," she argued, defiantly raising her chin as she spoke.

"El had provided, my wife," Abram explained. "Or have you forgotten that El allowed your suggestion that I take your servant to provide us an heir?"

"No, I have not forgotten. But it was a mistake," Sarai said in a decisive tone.

"A… mistake?" Abram asked confusedly.

Sarai saw her opening. "Yes! Hagar had too much pride, and she thought that she was our better," she said bitterly. "And now she is gone. Good riddance, I say."

"I understand that she was proud," Abram said quietly, waving his hand in the air, "and I think I know why. But I think she was also happy to be of service to us both."

This was more than Sarai could bear. "You have no idea. She bragged to the other servants that she could do something her mistress could not. I have not liked her from the beginning. Now you know why. Anyway," Sarah said, "it is now in the hands of El."

Abraham quickly debated whether or not to express his thoughts to Sarai. Finally, he nodded his head and said, "Did you drive her away, my wife?"

Sarah paused. "As I said; it is now in the hands of El." Abraham nodded again. He was used to Sarah's non-answer answers, but this time her evasiveness angered him.

"No," Abram said loudly, thinking of the young woman, the unborn child inside her, and the possible dangers she now faced. "This…this is on you, my wife."

SIXTEEN

The water tasted metallic to Ramla, but she didn't care. The wilderness on the way to Egypt had been unforgiving; the nights colder than she had remembered them being. Her companions were searing heat by day and frigid winds at night. There were times during those nights when she remembered the warmth of Sarai's tent with longing, but the memories of the beating she received quickly squashed those thoughts. Freezing was better than being beaten. But now, she knew, the worst was over. Ahead of her, Shur, the traditional border of eastern Egypt, waited only a day or so away.

Ramla immediately felt tired, her thirst quenched by the water, so she found a level, shady place under one of the few palms that surrounded the small oasis and stretched out for a rest out of the way of the other travelers who came to get water for themselves and their animals. The morning sun was not too hot yet, and although she could make some good time before the midday sun, she decided the rest would do her good. That's when she heard the voice.

"Ramla, where are you going?" the voice said, in her native tongue.

Ramla sat straight up, surprised that someone had come upon her without her knowing it. It then struck her that the voice had used her name.

"Who's there?" she asked quietly, but then, immediately, deep inside her, she knew.

It was El.

She answered immediately. "I'm running away from Sarai and from her service. I'm going home to have my child there," she stated without emotion. In her heart, she knew that the God wanted complete candor, for who can keep secrets from the Gods?

She thought, as she said the words, that the voice sounded exactly as Abram said it did: Calm, young, but powerful.

It also crossed her mind that she was dreaming, but she had not had time to fall asleep when the voice spoke. She quickly noted that, yes, she was still at the oasis, so this was no dream. Then, the voice spoke again.

"I need you to return to Abram and Sarai," the voice said.

The words struck Ramla like a blow. Yet, in her heart, she knew better than to defy such a God as this.

"Your place is not in Egypt; it is where I have put you," the voice continued. "Go back there and humble yourself before your master and mistress."

Ramla stood and stretched her arms in front of her, her palms facing upwards, as she did years before in the presence of the Goddess. "Yes, my Lord. I will do as you say."

"And do not be afraid; I will give you the promise I made to Abram, because of him. You will be the mother of many people.

The child inside you is a son. I have heard your distress. I know how deeply hurt you are—inside and out. You will name the son Ishmael because he will remind you that El has heard your trouble," the voice said.

Ramla, keeping her arms out and palms up, kneeled and bowed in reverence. The voice paused.

She answered, her own voice betraying the amazement she felt. "You are the God Who Sees Me. You see me even out here in the desert. You must be the God of Gods."

"I will be with you; I will protect you. The child is a child of the promise. Do not forget that," the voice added.

Ramla, still with bowed head and body, began swaying and chanting a prayer of thanksgiving. "I will never forget it, my Lord. Never. May El be praised! My heart sings to you, oh El. Your servant will do as You say. My home is where You send me. My work is to do as You instruct me. I thank You for Your caring watchfulness over me, oh God of Abram!"

The wind suddenly began whipping the oasis sand as it had done at the clearing when Ramla had witnessed the covenant ceremony with Abram. And, as quickly as it came, the wind subsided with a rush. But Ramla knew that the God Who Sees Me would never leave her.

She stood, suddenly filled with purpose and energy. Returning to the oasis, she filled her water skin, slung it around her shoulder, and began the journey back towards Abram, Sarai, and home.

SEVENTEEN

Against the background of the early dawn, Ramla saw the outline of Abram's tents in the compound ahead of her. Then Ramla spied the figure of a man coming towards her. She knew from the silhouette that it could only be Abram. He approached her quickly.

"My lord, why are you outside the camp so early?" Ramla asked, noticing that his face could not hide a look of relief.

"Why, I was looking for you, my child. Did you lose your way while out walking?" Abram tried to give the poor young woman an excuse, at least. He saw that her clothes were dirty and her hair matted. She had thrown off the head covering somewhere along the way.

As it was in the desert, so it was with Abram; it was not in Ramla's nature to lie. "No, sir. I ran away. I was going back to Egypt, but now I am back where I am supposed to be. I'm sorry that I worried you, sir. I would never want to purposely hurt you of all people."

The pair walked side by side back into the camp. A few servants were stirring, preparing the morning meals and gathering water to begin the day. They straightened up from their work as the old man and the young, pregnant woman walked by them. The pair stopped not far from Sarai's tent.

"Ramla, I…" Abram began. He turned towards her and she to him. Abram couldn't bring himself to tell her how much he worried about her.

Ramla stood with her head bowed, the brown skin of her cheeks turned even darker by her time in the sun while running away from Abram's group. The tears began to stream down them. She cut him off as he paused. "I can't lie to you, sir. She beat me. I left."

Her honesty brought a slight smile to his face. "Here, here," Abram said soothingly, trying to comfort her. He reached out to her and grabbed her thin shoulders, small clouds of desert dust rising from them when he touched them. "It will be fine. All is well. As you say, you are back where you belong." He looked up from her to see the flap from Sarai's tent close, and he knew then that his wife had seen his gesture of kindness.

"And the child within you? All is well?" he asked.

She nodded and, with a smile through her tears, said. "Yes, my lord; your boy is fine."

"My boy?" he said, smiling even broader. "Your Goddess told you this?"

"Oh, sir!" Ramla began, suddenly remembering what had happened to her in the desert. "I have so much to tell you! I spoke with El. El spoke with me! Yes, El told me that we will have a male child. And I am also of the promise, El said."

Abram wrinkled his nose and tried to understand what the young woman was telling him. "What do you mean—you 'spoke with El'? Do you mean you heard El speak? Tell me, please!"

"Yes. I heard the voice, as do you. Yes, I will...I will tell you all," she said.

"Ah, yes, well," Abram said, a bit startled at the news. "But first, we must make this right with my wife. You owe her that, at least."

"Yes, sir. I owe her that. At least."

"You realize that you have done what she said you would do, don't you?" Abram didn't have to tell Ramla whom he meant. She nodded slowly, looking into Abram's face. "You have become the Runaway—Hagar. You can't undo that now. What you can do, with the help of El, is do your best to be the bearer of El's promise to me and to all of us. And I insist you tell me what El said to you in the desert."

She nodded in agreement. "I will, my lord. You have my word."

Abram continued. "Ramla, I will make a promise of my own to you. I promise you this: If you make things right with my wife, I will give you your own tent, your own servants—your own household," Abram said.

Ramla couldn't believe her ears. "R...really?" she said, her eyes beginning to well with tears. Could it be? Could she be receiving blessings from El through Abram? Had the promise made in the desert already started to be fulfilled?

"Yes, certainly," Abram answered with a slight chuckle. "You think my wife could allow both you and the child to share her tent?" He looked at Ramla with raised eyebrows to see if she found his comment amusing.

"No," she managed with a smile and a snort through her tears, "She barely tolerates me alone!"

"Yes, I know. We will remedy that. But we must make things right with Sarai. Agreed?"

Ramla nodded. If all of this ended with having her own household, Ramla would do practically anything.

"And," Abram continued," I promise that I shall make you my wife."

"Oh, sir!" Ramla gushed, embracing the old man with a fierce grip of gratitude. "That would do me honor, my lord."

"No, my dear," he answered, pushing her away and looking into her brown eyes. "The honor is mine. But, first…" and he nodded towards Sarai's tent.

Abram took her by the hand and led Ramla into Sarai's tent. The older woman sat on her pillows but faced away from the door. It was as if she was forcing Ramla to come around in front of her, as if she didn't want to make this easy on Ramla at all.

"What do you have to say for yourself?" Sarai ordered when the pair had made their way in front of her.

"What do you have to say to your mistress?" Abram echoed, but his words were kinder, more encouraging than scolding.

Ramla paused, but then got to her knees and bowed low before Sarai. With her face to the tent's carpet, she did not look at the older woman, but she sensed that Sarai wore her usual smug and self-satisfied smile.

"I am sorry for running away, mistress Sarai."

"And what else?" Abram asked, trying to sound stern for his wife's sake, even though his heart broke for Ramla.

Without looking up, Ramla said, "I am your servant. Please; call me Hagar."

PART II

HAGAR

ONE

Sarai's absence from the wedding feast was noted. Of course, few of the servants and families expected her to show up for the marriage festival that celebrated Abram's taking Hagar as a wife. The ceremony between the two of them took place a month before the birth of the child, and Abram had invited all the neighboring tribesmen and kings of the cities of the valley. Melchizedek, too, came, and offered his blessing on the union, even breaking protocol by placing his hands on her stomach and making a prayer of gratitude, much to the delight of Hagar but causing gossip among the others assembled.

For the ceremony, Hagar managed to put together a passable wedding ensemble for herself, borrowing woven sandals and even managing to find and wear the traditional eye makeup of her home country—which made her already smoky eyes wider, lovelier, and darker still. All the crowd remarked how beautiful she looked.

Eliezer had worked hard to find what she said she needed for the ceremony, and Hagar thanked him profusely. "It is my honor because of Abram. Now, as his wife, keep his honor yourself," he said after dropping off a fine piece of bead-worked cloth Hagar could use as a head covering during the ceremony.

"I would not think to do otherwise, kind sir," Hagar answered.

"I know," he said, and smiled as he left her tent.

Abram had kept his word to Hagar. Her first night back from the desert, she had her own tent on the opposite side of the compound from Sarai; Abram saw to that himself. The next morning, Eliezer had appointed a young girl to be her own servant. She had been given the name Bracha. She was a mute orphan who had wandered into camp a few years earlier and who was being raised more as a child of the entire community rather than any one individual family's responsibility.

"Bracha?" Hagar said, repeating the young girl's name when Eliezer brought the child in and introduced them. "We know each other, don't we? Your name; that means, 'Blessing', right?" she said, smiling at the girl. Bracha, her light skin and ruddy hair a bit dirty, smiled back broadly with a slight bow. "We will get along fine," Hagar said, thanking Eliezer for his wisdom. When he had left, Hagar said to Bracha: "So. We are both orphans, I understand. Well, we will see about making our home together, shall we?"

The silent girl beamed. Ramla continued: "Soon, we will welcome another here with us—my son. You will help me with him, won't you?" Bracha nodded vigorously, and her smile could not possibly grow wider.

"I am Hagar," she added. At this, Bracha cocked her head slightly, her smile turning into a slight grimace. Hagar explained. "Yes, I know what you're thinking. I used to be Ramla, but since

I have run away and now returned I am now known as Hagar, I suppose." The girl smiled again, her fair eyes grew wide, and she nodded animatedly, pointing at herself. Ramla's eyes narrowed, then she understood and smiled. "Ah! You, also, are a runaway. Then you are a 'Hagar,' too. Yes, I suppose many of us are."

"Well," Hagar said with a slight laugh, "there will be no more running away by either one of us, will there? Let's see what needs to be done in here," she said, turning around and looking at the largely empty tent. So, the two of them together began to make order of their new home.

Bracha, who had a reputation in the camp of being somewhat slow witted, proved to be quite the opposite. Hagar found her to be a quick learner, bright, and curious. Hagar also felt in her heart that Bracha also had the gift of discernment of the will of the Gods and said as much to her one evening after supper in their first few days together.

"Bracha, I must ask you, do you know about things before they happen? What I mean is do you sometimes see things about other people that they don't know anyone else knows or that they don't know themselves?" The girl wrinkled her turned-up nose slightly and looked around uncomfortably. Hagar understood. "It's alright, Bracha. I didn't understand the gift myself. When I was your age, those feelings that I had been given made me not liked by other children. Do not fear this gift. It is from El to you. Don't be shy then; tell me."

Bracha, her eyes watering, nodded slowly. Her mouth opened to speak, but no words came. Then, tensing her shoulders and pursing her lips, she placed her fingertips on her forehead and closed her eyes. Suddenly, she opened her eyes wide and threw her fingers out and open from her head. "Yes!" Hagar said, agreeing. "It is like the images burst from your head. That is a good way of saying it." Bracha grinned, thrilled to be understood by someone at last. "We will talk more of this," Hagar said, "but for now, help me get these pots out to wash."

The same week she returned from the desert, Abram sent word that he wished to speak to Hagar in his tent. Without asking, Bracha accompanied Hagar, almost running to keep up with Hagar's long-legged strides as she made her way to Abram's quarters. The pair found Abram alone, sitting on his cushions and drinking some new wine. He waved them in when they opened the tent flap and bade them to sit on the cushions opposite him.

"I see that you two are getting along well," he said to Hagar, nodding and smiling at Bracha as they took their places.

The girl smiled and nodded as Hagar said, "Oh, yes, sir! We have become fast friends. And," Hagar said, leaning in a bit towards Abram, "she, too, has the gift. We are finding that there is more to learn from each other."

This delighted Abram, and he said, "I must thank Eliezer for recommending this arrangement. The man is worth every bit I pay him." Glancing at Hagar and then down at his wine cup, he then asked, "How do you feel, my child? You look as if you are almost to term."

"Well! I seem to have gained strength from my walk that will sustain me during childbirth. For that, I am grateful to El," Ramla explained. "Yes; I think in a few weeks at most."

"I am pleased you mention El," Abram said, looking up at her again. "Now, I want you to tell me about your experience in the desert."

Hagar closed her eyes and nodded. She tried to bring back the feeling she had under the palms at the oasis. She imagined the whipping wind and the clarity of the calm, strong, young voice. "El knew that I was running away, but I think He tested me. He asked me what I was doing. I told him and why I was doing it. El then told me that Egypt," Hagar paused here and swallowed hard as if she were still trying to come to terms with the idea, "was no longer my home. That my home was here with you and my mistress, Sarai."

Abram beamed at this, but Hagar didn't see it through her closed eyes. She continued. "El then assured me that I will have a son and that he, like you, my master, will be the father of many people."

At this, Abram could not help but interrupt. "El be praised!" he said loudly. Bracha, startled by this outburst, looked from the old man to Hagar with her wide eyes. Hagar continued.

"I told El my surprise that even in the desert He could see me. El said that He knew of my suffering," Hagar paused again, the pain of Sarai's actions still fresh in her heart, "at the hands of my mistress."

Abram nodded. "El is the God who sees," he said. This comment finally caused Hagar to open her eyes and, blinkingly, look directly at Abram.

"Yes! He is the God Who Sees Me; He is the God Who Hears," she said with conviction. Abram's face became wet with joyous tears. Hagar smiled at him with warmth and affection. His obvious happiness at having a son was yet another proof to her heart that the choice she made was one that had pleased El.

"So, for me, my lord, El is now God Who Sees Me," she said, her heart and eyes filled with the confidence that this God was now her Protector and Champion.

Abram thought about this for a moment, turning his head to the side and looking at the carpet on the tent floor. Finally, as if he had convinced himself of something, he nodded to the carpet, looked up, and asked, "And the voice?"

Now it was Hagar's turn to nod. "It is exactly as you have said. And He spoke my name."

Abram stood. "Bracha," and the girl leapt to her feet, "take care of your mistress. Come get me if she is ready to have the child. I don't think it is quite yet. But just in case…" Bracha nodded eagerly. Abram smiled warmly at Hagar and bowed his head slightly. "The wedding will be within the week. We have sent for all to come. Ask Eliezer for anything you might need.

Hagar and Bracha then left Abram's quarters to return to Hagar's tent. It took Hagar a few minutes to realize that Sarai had not been mentioned in the conversation.

Sarai stayed in her tent for many days and, other than her new servant girl coming and going to get food or to throw out the chamber pot for her mistress, no one saw or heard from her for several days before or after the wedding. Then immediately before the child was to be born, she was heard from again.

"It is simply not done," Sarai insisted when Abram told her of his intention to be in the birthing tent when Hagar's baby would be born. "She thinks herself above us already," she reminded him with sharpness narrowing her eyes. "You mustn't honor her with your presence."

Yet, Abram would not be swayed. "I am not trying to give her honor, my beloved," Abram said, trying to soothe Sarai's fears. "At least any more than a wife of mine deserves, do you not agree? Besides, I want to see our child when he first comes."

"How do you know her offal will be a boy?" Sarai asked sharply. "Besides, I do not want anything to do with that woman's child."

"Ah, do not say that, my wife," he half soothed and half scolded, "since that 'offal' as you call it is mine as well." Then, his anger getting the better of his reason, he reminded her, "I must remind you of your promise. Regardless of your protests, you must keep your word. You have sworn to raise this child as your own." He said this knowing Sarai's outburst that followed was inevitable.

"That will never happen!" Sarai screamed, and angrily turned over a bowl of figs that had been brought to her by the girl who had taken Hagar's place. Abram turned away and walked out of the tent, followed by Sarai's curses on his back. Abram was sure the entire camp had heard her. He silently chided himself for broaching the subject in the first place. Yet, he was determined to see the child born.

Hagar's labor had not been a long one. The older servant woman who was the midwife for the encampment assisted with the birth and told Abram through smiling, crinkled eyes, "I've seen far, far worse." Then, turning and addressing Hagar she said, "You were lucky." Taking a sharp, handleless blade, the midwife cut the umbilical cord from the bright red, crying infant, and placed it in a pan that Bracha held. "Yes, my lord; it is a male child," she said to Abram over her shoulder, although no question as to the gender of the newborn had been asked by anyone.

When the woman raised the blood-smeared child into Abram's arms, the old man cradled the boy's head. Tears of joy streamed down his weathered face and through his beard and splashed into the brown-skinned child's eyes causing the boy to twist and writhe.

The sight made Abram laugh joyously, and he raised the squirming boy before his face. With a loud voice, he said, "Praise be to El, the God above all Gods. For he has kept His promise, and I am thankful and will be forever faithful to His Name. A son! Praise El! This is your doing, oh my God. Your servant humbly thanks you."

Abram looked down at Hagar as he lowered the child back to his chest. Hagar's own sweat and tears mingled, and her breathing had yet to return to normal. Yet, Abram smiled broadly at her as Bracha wiped at Hagar's head with a wet cloth. He nodded his head appreciatively to her and grinned at Hagar.

"And I thank you, my child. Thank you. May God bless you for this." He looked back at the baby in his arms, holding the boy out from him. "And," Abram added with a laugh, "He has your eyes!" He turned quickly and walked out of the tent with the child, leaving the three women looking at each other wonderingly.

After the child was born, Abram gave Hagar two days in her tent alone with Bracha to be tended to and to rest. The midwife checked on Hagar on the first day to make sure there were no problems after the birth, and Hagar assured her that she was resting and was gaining back her strength. Hagar asked her, "Have you seen my son?" She had not even held him yet; Abram had taken the boy out immediately.

The woman looked at Bracha suspiciously and then remembered that the girl couldn't speak. So, in hushed tones, she said, "Yes; our master Abram has the child in Sarai's tent. A nursemaid has been brought in regularly. She has told me that Sarai doesn't like the baby."

This caused Hagar's heart to skip. She sat up on her cushions quickly and said loudly, "Doesn't like him? She won't hurt my son!" as tears began to swell her dark eyes.

The midwife shushed her into lying back down. Bracha came up quickly with a cup of water, and the midwife, supporting the back of Hagar's head, made her drink it. "There, there," she soothed. "All will be well. Master Abram will see to that." This seemed to calm Hagar, and she nodded. "You must rest. Get your strength back." Standing and turning to Bracha, she said, "Continue to give her water. Some soup would be good, too. Solid food later if she can take it. If your mistress has any pain or bleeding, be sure to come find me, do you understand?" The girl's head bobbed up and down quickly. "Good girl!" she said, patting the child's cheek, and left the tent.

Hagar slept. Bracha stayed close to her all through that day and night, sitting with her knees clasped before her. She watched as Hagar dreamed and slept fitfully. Every time Hagar woke, Bracha gave her something to drink. Hagar always took it with thanks and the pair exchanged small smiles.

Abram brought the child in the next morning. Bracha was brushing Hagar's dark hair as Hagar was eating some bread and fruits, the first real food she felt like taking since the birth. She quickly threw it aside when Abram silently bent down to give the child to her to hold. For Hagar, the moment was magical. The face of her mother flashed in her head as she whispered a small prayer to El.

"You're right, my lord," she said with tears of joy to Abram as she pulled back the small blanket to see her child's face for the first time. "He has my eyes." Bracha bent down behind Hagar's shoulder to get a better look at the small bundle.

Abram's eyes twinkled with his own tears. "I think the boy should be with his mother, don't you?" he asked.

"You...you mean, with me?" Hagar asked, not believing her ears. "But what of mistress Sarai's promise to raise him as her own?"

"Hagar, you of all people know my wife almost as well as I do. She would never keep your child. Her anger and pride won't allow it. I love her. You know that. But she is what she is, and that will never change. No, this is your son. You must raise him until he is of age for him to be with me and the other men."

Abram looked down at the trio below him and then around the tent at the accoutrements. He smiled and sniffed. "You seem to have done well in here in such a short time. Bracha, can you help mistress Hagar with the baby?" The girl looked up from the child for a moment and nodded, smilingly. "I know you will." He sat on cushions near Hagar and continued. "Do you need a wet nurse, Hagar? The camp has several…"

Hagar shook her head. "No," she said in a calm tone. "That I will do myself."

Abram seemed satisfied with this. He is a hungry little man, but if you feel you can, that is a good thing." Then, getting to his point, leaning forward on his cushions, he said: "Now that's settled. Let's talk about the boy's name."

At this Hagar immediately said, "Oh, I already know. Ishmael."

Both Bracha and Abram took their eyes off the child and looked at her. Bracha nodded. Abram put a hand to his beard and stroked it, thinking. "Hmm, 'God hears'; yes. It is fitting. Agreed!" he said with finality.

"It is the name God-Who-Sees-Me agreed to in the desert," she added. Abram looked at her with an awed smile. Hagar continued. "And I have another request, my lord," Hagar said, still not taking her eyes off the boy.

"Yes, of course. What is it you need?"

Hagar hesitated for a moment. She then looked up from the

boy to Abram's face. "I want the midwife to come soon and help me. I wish circumcision for my son."

Abram slowly blinked twice. He knew that such was the practice among the Egyptians, but it had never been performed in his homeland as far as he knew. Hagar saw him thinking and added, "It is our custom to do so. It is better for the man, cleaner, and safer. I know you want what is best for our son, my lord."

The thought still caught Abram by surprise. Finally, he said, "I can't think of a reason to say no to your request. You say it is better for the male children?"

"Cleaner, certainly, my master," Hagar said, cooing at the boy who slept soundly in her arms. "And it is safer, too. As a favor to me, sir," she added, looking up at Abram.

"I will see to it that the midwife comes to you as soon as possible. I know she has a delivery today, so this may have to wait until another day," he said.

"I thank you, sir," Hagar nodded and turned back to Ishmael. "He is a good baby, isn't he, my lord?" she asked of Abram.

"Yes, I've noticed he is not a crier. But as I said before, he is a hungry fellow!" the old man laughed. Abram watched as Bracha blinked her pale eyes at the boy, and he smiled to himself at the joy Hagar seemed to have shining from her now that she had her son with her. The two women were so enthralled by the beautiful child that they did not notice when Abram slipped out of the tent.

TWO

A decade passed on bird's wings.

Hagar could barely think of a time when her beautiful brown boy was not laughing and playing around her all day. She grew into a contented peace in her place among Abram's family; the child and the fact that she was now a wife of Abram gave her status and respect among the community.

Ishmael grew sturdy and smart, if not overly tall for his age. Hagar convinced Abram to allow the boy to stay with her longer than other boys did with their mothers. Most boys were sent to work in the fields with the animals at an early age, but Ishmael stayed close to his mother's side until he was over seven years old. That was not to say he wasn't a worker; he busied himself running errands for his mother and most of the other women in the camp. As Abram's son, the boy was the favorite of all, except Sarai.

To be fair, Sarai did not seek out the child for scoldings and chidings. Yet, whenever Ishmael crossed her path, Sarai was sure to rain threats and curses on his head. On those times, the boy would return to his mother's tent with a tear or two on his face, and Hagar had to remind him again and again that there were simply some people in life who would never like you no matter what you did or didn't do. She always insisted that Ishmael show Sarai respect at all times, even if Sarai showed none herself. It was what God-Who-Sees-Me would want, after all, she told her son. To be otherwise would be impious.

When Abram finally insisted that Ishmael come into the fields with him, the lad found that he loved the pastures and woods. He came to care deeply for the animals and learned quickly to spot quality among the flocks. "Those are things that cannot be taught easily," Abram told Hagar when he brought a tired Ishmael home after one long day outdoors. "It is as if he were born into it. He will do well." Smiling at Hagar, he added, "I am proud of him," and lovingly patted his son on the head.

Moments such as those gave Hagar intense happiness, and she praised God-Who-Sees-Me for His love and care and blessings.

She also felt a sense of happiness about Bracha who had grown into a happy, if silent, young woman. The relationship had become much less a mistress-servant one and more like that of an older and younger sister. That was not to say that Bracha was not completely devoted to Hagar's service, but the younger woman loved Hagar and saw her work for her mistress as a joy and privilege.

Recently, Hagar had noticed how several young men looked at Bracha's red hair and fair skin and lovely pale eyes. She asked Bracha about marriage one evening as the pair readied supper. The mute young woman frowned deeply and shook her head with violence. She pointed at Hagar and then to her own heart.

And then she closed her eyes and beamed a toothy grin. Hagar understood. For Bracha, Hagar's tent was home, but Hagar wanted Bracha to know that she had been given the freedom to choose to marry if she found someone suitable and if Abram approved. But Bracha wouldn't hear of it.

For her part, Hagar, too, cared deeply for Bracha; in fact, next to her mother, Hagar never felt closer to a person than she did the young woman. Even though she was Abram's wife, the old man had never visited her tent in his capacity as a husband. While that fact never truly bothered Hagar, and given that Ishmael brought her such joy, Hagar still had days when she felt a sadness and isolation. In those moments, she became reminded that God-Who-Sees-Me was her true protector even if she were married to Abram. And she took comfort that her God had given her Bracha as a helper and as a salve to her loneliness.

Despite never visiting her bed, it was not that Abram neglected her care; no, the opposite was true. He made sure she had what she needed and more. Sometimes, he would send by Ishmael a gift of food or cloth or some small, fine bowl or trinket, saying, "Give this to your mother, my son."

So, Hagar made sure she treasured every day as she woke to a wonderful God, a caring husband, a beautiful, healthy son, and a good sister whom she loved and who loved her dearly.

Ishmael had recently turned 12 when El spoke to Abram again.

"Abram," El said one night as the old man slept, "Wake. Come with me." Abram jolted up, grabbed a stick, and followed the voice out of his tent. When he had walked away from the camp, El told him to stop a moment. "My covenant with you," El said, "is still strong. I want you to be true to it. Here is a sign for you to wear that you are the chosen one of my covenant. Circumcise every male—slave and free—in your company. That will be a sign for you and your descendants for generations to come."

"Yes, my Lord; I shall do it," Abram promised. In respect, he knelt on the ground and then laid his full body, face down, before the voice of El.

"You remember my promises to you?" El asked. Abram's heart answered that he did, deeply and truly. "Good!" El said. They are true. Trust. Believe. Your children will be kings and will be my children forever. Nations will come from you, and peoples not yet born will call on your name."

The words sent a shock of thrill throughout Abram's body, but El was not finished.

"And you. You will no longer be merely an honored father; you will be the father of many nations. Call yourself Abraham," El commanded. "And Sarai; she will be an even greater princess; call her Sarah, for many nations will come from her as well."

"Lord my God," Abram said, his face still to the ground, "Sarai...Sarah...is almost 90 now. Thank you for Ishmael, however. He will praise you forever. Thank you for blessing him!"

"No, no!" El said, the calm voice rising slightly with emphasis. "Sarah will have a child in a year. I know your heart laughs at the prospect of such a thing. So, to remind you that anything is possible with me, give the name Isaac to the son she has."

El continued. "Ishmael will be great. Twelve princes will come from him, truly, but I will bless Isaac more."

"El be praised," was all Abram could say, the promise of El practically taking his breath away. He looked up and saw that the daylight was breaking over the tents to the east of where he was.

He stood and, grabbing his staff, quickly made his way to the tent of Eliezer. He meant to honor his commitment to El to circumcise all the men and boys in his charge as soon as possible. "Eliezer!" he yelled as he approached the tent, "get up! We have work to do!"

THREE

Abram told Eliezer about his conversation with El, but he didn't share it with Sarai. Hagar, knowing the signs and having the gifts she had, knew that something had occurred. Abram never made large decisions without El being involved. Circumcising the entire male population of the camp must have come only from God-Who-Sees-Me, she reasoned. She said as much to Abram a few weeks later.

"What else did El tell you, master?" she asked casually one day when she and Bracha brought bread and water to Abram, Ishmael and the men with them in that particular meadow.

Abram's face wore a shocked expression when she asked. He then narrowed his aged eyes, looked at Hagar, and cocked his head. He said, "Ah, so you know, then?" Hagar nodded and smiled. "El reassured me about the promises. He asked that I honor the covenant with the circumcision of all the males. It seems, Hagar, you were right about that." Hagar waved her hand as if that were of no consequence.

"But there was something else, too, wasn't there?" she asked. Then, realizing that her questions might be probing so deeply that she might have offended Abram, she said, "My lord, if this is too close to your heart to say...forgive me."

Abram looked up from her to see Ishmael and Bracha sitting in the grass, sharing a piece of bread and a water skin. He grimaced slightly. "I can tell you," he said softly so that no one else could hear. "El promised me another son." Before Hagar could register her surprise at this, Abram added quickly, "By Sarai."

It was Hagar's turn to look at their son. She bit her lower lip to keep from laughing and then smiled. The thought of Sarai having a child seemed absurd.

"That sounds...unusual, my lord, but with the God-Who-Sees-Me, anything is possible."

Abram continued to talk in hushed tones. "I thought so, too. And, there is more. Since El has promised me that I will be the father of many, He has changed my name to Abraham. Sarai, a princess, now will be even more of a princess. Her name is to be Sarah."

Hagar looked up at Abram. "It is a good name, my lord, I am pleased...for you and my mistress, Sarah—both." She bowed to him and went to join her son and Bracha on the grass. She wondered why her master would keep such wonderful news a secret for so long, but then, she reasoned, everyone would react the way she herself did when she heard. They, too, would laugh at an almost 90-year-old woman having a child. And, with Sarah's personality... she didn't seem like the nurturing type. People laughing at how strange the whole situation would be would hurt the old man deeply. No, Abraham's pride wouldn't take such a thing easily, especially concerning his beloved Sarah.

The next day, Abraham sat in the doorway of his tent in the heat of the day, resting and enjoying a small meal after having spent the morning chasing shepherds to get an accurate count of his flocks. Three young, beardless men, unannounced or unaccompanied by any servant, walked up towards his tent. Suddenly, the realization of exactly who these men might be struck him in his heart.

Abraham got to his feet and ran to meet them, throwing himself on the ground before them. "Oh, my Lords!" he said stretching his full frame on the ground in reverence. "You bless your servant by coming here! Allow me to serve you now, please."

"Yes," said one of the men, the taller of the three, who seemed to be the leader. "If you wish to serve us, please go ahead and do what you will." The man's voice sounded like that of El, Abraham thought, although it did not quite have the power in it that Abraham had become used to.

Abraham leapt to his feet and called for a servant to bring water. A young woman nearby quickly brought two pitchers, one on each shoulder, and another, younger girl, brought a wide basin and some clean towels.

"Wash their feet," he ordered. "Give them water. Give them anything they ask for."

To the men, he said, "Let us go under the shade of that tree there, and you can rest." Abraham motioned to a nearby oak, one of the larger ones on Mamre's land that shaded Abraham's tent in the later afternoon. As the men and the servants moved towards the tree, Abraham ran as fast as he could to Sarah's tent and almost tripped over the flap in his haste.

"My wife, get your servant to make fresh bread. Quickly!"

Sarah moved as if in a trance. She was allowing her servant girl to brush her long hair and didn't want to be disturbed. Her lack of understanding frustrated Abraham. He repeated his order. "Wife! Now! Bread! Quickly! Messengers from El are here!" Without waiting for her, he turned and headed towards the edge of the compound where a young man was bringing some animals into camp for the preparation of the evening meal.

"Noam, you need to take one of these, the best one, and prepare it to eat immediately."

The young man hesitated and looked confused. "These are for the supper, my lord."

Abraham shook his head. "No, my son. Prepare one of them now. Hurry! And bring the meat to the large oak near my tent. Waste no time, Noam!" The young man sprang into action, immediately taking one of the sheep, grabbing a short-handled knife from his waist, and slitting the animal's throat to drain the blood. Abram nodded in approval and hurried back to the three strangers.

The meal came together quickly. Fresh curds, the bread brought out by Sarah's servant girl, and the succulent lamb proved to be exactly what the three visitors wanted. They smacked their lips and licked their fingers appreciatively. Abraham stood by the tree as they ate, his mind and heart racing. When they finished the meal, they thanked Abraham, and he bowed to them in honor.

"Where is your wife, Sarah?" the tall one of the trio asked.

"She is in her tent, my Lord."

Abraham looked towards Sarah's tent and saw her standing in the doorway, listening to the conversation. He smiled at her, and she ducked her head back inside.

"Ah," the tall one said, looking in the direction Abraham looked. "I have news for you. This time next year, we shall come back this way again. And Sarah, your wife, will have a son by that time."

From the oak, Abraham could hear the loud laugh that Sarah gave when she overheard this news. He knew from the tone that the laugh was sarcastic and bitter.

The three young men looked at each other. One of the men, the one who looked the youngest, asked, "Why did she laugh?" Abraham blushed in embarrassment at the question. "Bring her here," he ordered.

Abraham called out, "Sarah…come…please. Meet these men of El."

Sarah strode proudly out of her tent, her chin held high. She came beside Abraham, and, as he introduced her, she did not bow or show obeisance.

"My wife, my Lords."

"Why did you laugh when you heard that you will have a child next year at this time?" the tall one asked of Sarah immediately.

"I didn't laugh. You are mistaken."

Abraham's face wore a shocked expression. This was too much, even for Sarah. The young men looked at each other again. The spokesman paused and then gently said, "Yes, we heard you laugh. True, you are beyond the age that women usually have children. But with El, all things are possible."

The phrase brought a thrill to Abraham's heart, but Sarah was still too proud to admit that she had laughed. Confronted with her lie, she also felt a bit of fear.

"I…I think it is ridiculous for a woman my age to have a child."

"Nevertheless, you will. A year from now."

Attempting to cover for Sarah, Abraham abruptly said, "Praise be to El!"

The three men stood. As they did, Abraham and Sarah moved back slightly, both of them now filled with awe and a bit of fear.

"We must be going. Thank you for the meal," the younger man said.

"I...I will escort you out of the camp," Abraham offered. Meanwhile, Sarah, her pride somewhat sullied, walked slowly back to her tent, but this time her chin was on her chest in thought.

As the group made its way out of camp, Abraham called for skins of water to be brought to the men. They took them from the servants with thanks and slung them over their shoulders.

"We will be going on to Sodom," the tall one said. "We want to see the city for ourselves."

"Ah, Sodom, yes; my nephew, Lot, lives there with his family."

"Yes, so we have heard. We thank you for your hospitality, Abraham. You will be blessed. Do not doubt it."

Abraham saw the men to the trail that led east and watched them until they were out of sight. As he returned to camp, his heart filled with wonder and joy at a God Who could make anything possible.

Then, Abraham realized that he had not brought Hagar to meet the men. He winced at the thought of this oversight. Surely, though, she would understand. As much as she would have wanted to greet the strangers, she would know that the prophecy concerned Sarah, not her. Besides, he reasoned, Hagar had an ongoing dialogue with God-Who-Sees-Me, while his precious Sarah seemed to have no such relationship.

And Hagar proved him right. She felt no slight or disrespect when he told her about the visit later. "Oh, my lord, I am so happy for you…and for mistress Sarah! A child! It is confirmed then. This time next year?"

"Yes, it is what the men said."

She nodded. "And," she paused, "what did mistress Sarah say?"

"She…found it difficult to believe…at first." He told her about Sarah's cynical laughter.

Again, Hagar smiled. "I am sure. Well, it is hard to believe. I would be inclined to find it so as well. But God-Who-Sees-Me is a God of the promise. She knows this, in her heart, I am sure."

"Perhaps. We will see. In any case, the three are on their way to Sodom. That is troubling to me."

"That they are going, or…"

"No," Abraham corrected her, "that they will not find people in Sodom who honor El. Including, I'm afraid, Lot."

Hagar saw the deep lines of worry crease Abraham's brow when he said this. "What," she swallowed deeply as she, too, began to be concerned, "do you think will happen, my lord?"

"I fear El will punish the city."

Abraham's words hung heavily in the air for a moment. Then, Hagar gasped. "Oh, my lord! God-Who-Sees-Me is merciful and compassionate," she said, looking at Bracha and Ishmael as they sat playing together in the tent. "I know this. He will not destroy them, my lord."

"I don't know," Abraham said. "Yes, El is all those things. But He is also a God who will not tolerate complete selfishness in His creation. This I know. This we both know. And that includes in us, Hagar."

She agreed. "Selfishness is ingratitude, isn't it, my lord?" she asked.

"Why, yes; yes, it is. And Lot and his wife and children, they chose Sodom for a home because of the way the people there live. I fear that my relatives are that type of people. You said it well: Ungrateful."

The pair stood in silence a moment. Then, Hagar's eyes brightened with an idea. "My master, why don't you ask El to spare Sodom if He could find grateful people there?"

Abraham mulled this possibility. "Yes," he said, pulling on his beard in thought. "It is a good thing you have said. I shall do so."

FOUR

L ot often joined the men of the city as they sat at the city gate in the late afternoons. It was the perfect place to see everyone and to catch up on the latest news or gossip. The men shared stories and laughter and, most often, sat bragging about their latest trades or romantic conquests. Lot learned quickly that one needed a thick skin to take the joking and friendly derision that happened there.

Life had returned to normal in Sodom for some time since the war that had taken most of the population away into slavery. The war was rarely mentioned anymore; it became more of a marker of time than a lesson or cautionary tale. The king was still the king. Trade and enjoying the moment had become the hallmarks of the city. It was one of the things Lot and his wife, Ado, liked about the city. The people enjoyed life. Almost every evening ended with drinking and feasting and a party with music and dancing.

Ado took pleasure in the fine cloth and trinkets and good food that wound their way into Sodom because of the trade routes along the river leading to the sea. She enjoyed watching her daughters dress in thin, expensive cloth, and laughingly comparing their beauty in the clothes. And, recently, she and Lot had found sons of wealthy men as suitable husbands for their two daughters. She and her girls busied themselves with plans for the impending weddings. For Ado, life in Sodom was good. She tried to forget the loneliness and crude surroundings of life following Abram and his God.

As Lot sat laughing and swapping stories with the men at the city gates one evening, two young men approached in a throng of travelers and traders. Even at a distance, something about the men stirred a feeling in Lot, and he stopped listening to the other men's stories and watched the approaching two strangers. "Lot, did you hear that last bit?" a friend of Lot's said as he noticed Lot's attention drawn away.

"No. Sorry. No. I'll be right back, Keret" Lot said to his friend. He got up and made his way towards the approaching pair. He intercepted them a few steps from the gate.

"Sirs!" he began. "Do I...do I know you?" Something about the men gnawed at Lot's stomach. The two young men looked at one another, then at Lot, and smiled at him.

"Perhaps," the younger of the pair said.

"Yes, yes, I do, I think. You are messengers; you have been sent from my uncle Abram's God, El, haven't you?"

The men nodded at Lot. He continued. "Please, sirs; come stay at my house tonight. We will feast. Ado, my wife, she will have our servants care for your every need."

The older looking of the two men answered. "We thought we would sleep in the marketplace in town tonight."

"Oh, sirs, no. Please. If you are of Abram's God, then please come to my house."

The men agreed, and the three of them made their way past the gates as the sun began to dip below the horizon. As they passed the gathering of men at the gate, one of Lot's companions yelled out, "Lot! Who are your friends? Where have you been hiding these beauties, eh?" The assembled crowd of men howled in laughter and began catcalling and whistling.

Lot blushed and sheepishly apologized to the two young men. "They are only making crude jokes. They mean no harm, sirs," he said.

Ado seemed more thrilled to have an excuse to have a party than to take care of the guests; of course, she needed little by way of excuse to make free with the wine and food almost nightly. She invited some neighbors to join them for the meal, telling them to be sure to bring some wine of their own.

The servants set up the low tables in a squared shape and prepared the evening's festivities while Lot had them bring water for the young men's feet and wine for their palates. As the family, the other guests, and the strangers sat on the cushions in the courtyard and watched the bustle of readiness before them, Ado and Lot's two daughters, newly engaged to be married, cut their eyes at the attractive young strangers.

Enkidu, the fiancé of Lot's oldest daughter, noticed the attention the girls were giving to the young men. "Here, Donatiya," he said, loudly addressing his betrothed who lounged at his side, "these men are much too pretty for you." He took a moment and looked at the strangers for himself. "For me, however…" he added, his voice trailing off with a smile. The girl slapped him hard but playfully, causing the young man to laugh even more. Hurriya, Lot's other daughter, and her fiancé, Yarih, joined in on the laughter. Soon, the neighbors, getting the joke, also laughed uproariously. All of this made Lot uncomfortable; he had become used to the coarseness of Sodom, but, in the presence of these men from El, even he knew that the joking was inappropriate.

As the bawdy laughter and even more comments continued, the two strangers looked gravely at each other with slight, knowing nods that were imperceptible to everyone present except Lot. He turned to his children with furrowed eyebrows and pursed lips as if to say, "Stop." His daughters saw his look and knew that they needed to show a bit more decorum before the guests, and, for that, Lot was grateful. The fiancés, however, and many of the other guests, still made the odd inappropriate joke during the meal, most of them about the anatomies of Lot's daughters.

During the end course, the younger foursome drifted off from the tables without a word to the adults. Ado, dribbles of spilled wine on her garment, began asking in a slurred voice for the latest gossip from the neighborhood. One of the women spoke up immediately and said, "You mean other than the fact that you will be housing the two most desirable men in Sodom in your bed tonight, Ado?" Many of the men in the group began laughing loudly again, banging the low table with their wine cups in appreciation of the joke.

Suddenly, from outside, a noise coming from the street drowned out the laughter in Lot's courtyard. It caused the partygoers to exchange puzzled looks. Even Ado, in her drunken state, blinked her vapid eyes rapidly, trying to comprehend what she was hearing. "What in the world is that?" she managed to slur.

Again, the two young visitors looked at each other with knowing expressions. Lot, still taking his cues from them, rose from his cushions with trepidation and went to the door of his house to see the source of the commotion. He opened the door and looked out. What he saw filled him with fear and shock.

It seemed like the whole town was in the street in front of his house. The men from the gate that afternoon, the ones who had made the first crude jokes about the visitors, seemed to be leading the crowd. Several of them shouted to Lot, "Let's have the pretty young men!" and "Bring them out!"

This last phrase became taken up by the large crowd. "Bring them out! Bring them out! Bring them out!" they chanted in unison.

Lot was horrified. He closed the door of his house behind him quickly and threw his hands up into the air. "Brothers! Brothers!" he cried. "I beg you, do not do this thing. I... I have my daughters you can...have them."

The crowd began to hoot, yell and curse at this suggestion. Lot persisted. "These men," he yelled, quieting the crowd somewhat, "they are under my roof...they are my guests. Please...!" Then, he spied his friend, Keret, in the crowd near the front. "Keret, I beg you..." he pleaded.

Lot's words seem to enrage the crowd rather than convince them to leave. Keret turned around and spoke to the crowd. "This foreigner, this man, he is not one of us. He calls us 'brothers,' but he thinks he is better than us and can tell us how to behave! No one tells us what to do!"

Cries of, "Kill him!" began to ring through the street. Almost as one man, the crowd surged towards Lot's front door, clawing to get at him. At that moment, Lot knew that he would soon be dead.

Then, almost miraculously, his front door opened and hands from inside grabbed him by his robe and pulled him inside to safety. The door shut tightly at the precise moment the crowd pressed against it.

Gasping for breath, Lot turned and saw that it was the messengers from El who had saved him. As the crowd outside beat on his door, Lot managed to say, "Save us! What are we going to do?"

Suddenly, the beating ceased. In its place, Lot heard a howling coming from the men in the street, a howling like one would hear from a dog that had been suddenly and seriously injured.

"We have blinded them. They can't harm you now."

Lot looked at the young men incredulously. "What?"

"Listen to us. Anyone you care for in the city: Your daughters, any servants that you care about, your wife and even your future sons-in-law. Gather them up and get ready to leave immediately. Quickly! We are about to destroy the city because El is angry at the selfishness of the people."

Lot's eyes grew even wider with fear and shock. He ran back into his inner courtyard. The howling in the street was almost too much for him to bear. He found Ado still sitting on the cushions at the supper table, her hands covering her ears from the cacophony of sound coming from the street. The dinner party guests and even the servants had gone.

"Up!" He said to Ado, gathering a moment of clarity. "Gather our daughters. We must get out of this place, for El is about to destroy the city."

His wife shook her head and kept covering her ears, rocking back and forth and saying, softly, "No, no, no."

Lot slapped her, hard. She took her hands down and stopped the rocking and the shaking of her head, her eyes slowly focusing on her husband's face. "Did you hear me?" He asked.

She nodded and stifled a sob. "Yes...yes," she answered flatly. "Quickly!"

"Yes," she said, and rose to find her daughters.

As Lot ran into the living quarters, he found his sons-in-law lounging on the new short couches Ado had recently bought and still drinking from the neighbors' wine. One of them asked, "Tell us father; what is all that noise about?"

Lot told them what the men of El had said. They looked at each other with fake surprise on their faces, and then they burst into laughter, slapping their thighs and mocking Lot. "You must believe me! All of it is true!" This only served to make the drunken young men laugh harder.

Lot, realizing he was getting nowhere with the pair, moved on to the servants' quarters. There he found only one of Ado's servant girls. He ordered her to go to her mistress's room and start packing what she could.

He began to panic. The thought ran through his head, "There's not enough time to put all our money onto pack animals." He thought of all his hard work and the numerous business deals he had made, and he began to realize that it was all for nothing. So, for most of the night, Lot wandered from room to room, as if he were in a trance, realizing as he passed through each room that it would be the last time he would see this place and these things.

Shortly before dawn, Ado and the daughters, tears now streaming down their faces, sat in stunned silence in the courtyard, waiting for Lot to tell them what to do next. Lot finally wandered in and, with an expressionless face, sat between his daughters and stared out at nothing. The plates and jugs and cups from the previous evening's dinner lay strewn about them.

The messengers from El entered. "Lot. Come. It is time."

"Hmm?" he replied, staring into the space in front him.

"Father," Donatyia said to him softly, tearfully pulling on his sleeve. "The men are talking to you."

"Hmm?" he answered again. The enormity of the situation had proven too much for Lot to comprehend. His trance from the night before remained unbroken.

"Yes," said the older of the two messengers. "Come with me, Lot." He stood over Lot and reached down with an outstretched hand. Lot looked at it strangely, as if he had never seen a hand before. He looked up at the messenger.

"Come…with you?" he asked.

"That's right. We need to go now."

Lot reached up and absentmindedly put his hand in the young man's. With a daughter on each side, they all assisted Lot in standing again. Leading Lot by the hand, the six of them and Ado's servant girl silently walked out the back of the house into the alley behind. The howls and moans of the blinded citizens of Sodom had subsided somewhat but still persisted at a distance. The eastern sky was beginning to show streaks of light as the little group made its way out of the city towards the river and the rising sun.

FIVE

Tears of sorrow streamed down Abraham's face.

He stood on the ridge overlooking the river valley. The late afternoon sun behind him illuminated the scene below. Down and to his right he could see smoke and fire coming from two—no, three—no, four cities and towns as they lay in the river basin. He could not see the last city of the five, Bela, in the distance, but in his heart he knew that it, too, suffered the same fate as her four sisters. In his mind, he listed them: Sodom, Gomorrah, Admah, Zeboim, Bela. He was too far away to hear the anguished cries of the citizens, but the smoke and the glow of the flames told him all he needed to know of the destruction that El had rained on those cities.

Only two days before, Abraham had stood on that same spot overlooking the cities of the valley, and he begged his God to spare Sodom and the other cities as Hagar had suggested he do. "My Lord, if You can find a few good people in those cities, I ask that you spare them."

The voice of the Lord answered him and agreed. "Yes; if I can find a handful of good people, I will not destroy the cities. My two messengers are in Sodom now. They will see for themselves." Abraham had been satisfied with that interaction and stopped by Hagar's tent to tell her as much. She thanked him for letting her know, but, in her heart, she knew the worst.

The smoke and the fire in the distance gave Abraham the answer from God that he feared. As he stood on the ridge, Hagar, Bracha, and Ismael slowly approached him from behind. Hagar and Bracha glanced at each other as they drew near because they could hear his anguished sobs. It was Ishmael who first spoke as they reached him.

"Father, why are you crying?"

When they reached the edge of the ridge, they found the answer to Ishmael's question. Abraham turned and, with a great sigh, picked up his son and hugged him tightly. Hagar gently touched Abraham's arm as a gesture of comfort. Her heart, too, ached for the cities that were being destroyed.

"They are all gone," Abraham said through his tears. "Lot, his family, and all the peoples. All the cities. Gone."

Hagar tried to calm the old man. "Shh," she said as one would to a crying child. "We must trust that God-Who-Sees-Me has rescued your nephew and his family."

"Do you think it?" Abram asked, holding his son closer.

"I know it, my lord."

"Father," Ishmael said, trying to catch his breath, "you're squeezing me too tight."

Abraham released his clench, kissed Ismael's forehead as a blessing, and set him down next to his mother. "I know, my son. Your father is sorry."

"I am fine, father," the boy said smilingly. "I'm too big now for you to hold me anyway."

This made Abraham smile slightly. "Yes, yes, you are turning into a fine young man." He turned back towards the cities as the smoke of destruction drifted towards the heavens.

"There is nothing we can do now," Hagar said, divining his thoughts. "El has done what He has done. Let us go home."

Ishmael grabbed his father's hand and looked up at the tall old man. "Father, will you dine with us tonight?" Abraham nodded slightly and again gave his son a small smile.

Ishmael looked at his mother as a way of asking her if his invitation was appropriate. Now, it was Hagar's turn to smile at her son. "Yes, it will be very late when we get home, but I think Bracha and I can fix your father something that you both will enjoy. We would be honored if you would join us," she said to Abraham.

The women and the boy led Abraham away from the edge of the ridge and back towards their home. For some distance, none of them spoke. Their thoughts lay with the smoking cities of the river valley behind them.

The next morning, Hagar had slept later than usual because they had all stayed up so late over a somber supper. Bracha, for whom sleep always seemed to be a nuisance, was already awake and preparing something light to eat. Hagar looked about her and asked, "Bracha, where is Ishmael?" The young woman looked up from her work and shrugged.

"But was he here when you woke?" Hagar asked. Bracha nodded and made a motion that suggested the boy was out playing somewhere already. At that moment, Ishmael entered the tent followed by a grimy, exhausted-looking young girl about his age and whose hand he held.

"Mother, look who I found in the camp."

Hagar, still not quite awake, had to blink several times before she began to realize who the child was. "Why...you're Ado's servant girl..." She trailed off because the girl's name escaped her for the moment.

"Mother!" Ishmael scolded. "It's Yardena. You remember? We were friends before she went to work for Uncle Lot."

At hearing the names of her mistress and master, the girl dropped Ishmael's hand. Her eyes started welling with tears. Hagar suddenly realized the importance of the child's presence. "Lot! Where is he? Is his family well?" she asked, standing from her bed with a start and moving to the girl. Bracha dusted her hands on the front of her dress and came over also.

But all Yardena could do for the moment was weep. It was as if a dam had suddenly burst. She grabbed Hagar about the waist and sobbed uncontrollably into Hagar's side. With the girl not able to speak, Hagar looked at Ishmael. He was old enough to know something was wrong but not old enough to know what it could be.

"My son, where did you find her?"

"I went out to play before breakfast. You were still asleep. Yardena came walking into camp as if she were asleep herself. I said 'Hello, Yardena!' to her, but she didn't answer. Then, I took her by the hand and brought her straight here to you."

"You did well," Hagar said to Ishmael, stroking the dirty, matted hair of the frightened girl as she cried. Hagar gently pulled the child away from her leg and got down on her knees before her.

"Here," she said, "let's get a good look at you." Bracha ran and got a wet cloth and brought it back to Hagar. Wiping the girl's face of the grime and smokiness as well as her tears, Hagar soothed her.

"There, there, that's better. That's better, isn't it, Yardena? See? You're well."

The girl sniffed and tried to smile, but she only managed a slight grimace. Hagar continued to wipe her face and caress her hair, calming her as she would a frightened animal. Yardena began to tremble slightly as if she were cold, and she brought both of her fists to her mouth.

"Ishmael, run, go and fetch your father. Tell him it's about Lot."

Again, at hearing the name of her master, the girl let out a small sob. The boy ran out of the tent, and Hagar and Bracha began to fuss over Yardena in an effort to calm her. Hagar gently pulled her arms down from her mouth and told her, "Our master, Abraham, will be coming. Do you think you can talk to him, please?"

With an absent-minded stare, the girl nodded, still shivering slightly, as a single tear ran down her cheek. Bracha bent with a grin and deftly wiped it away with a thumb and then pinched the frightened girl's face lovingly. Yardena managed a small smile this time and Bracha beamed back at her.

After a moment, Ishmael returned with Abraham. "Here he is, mother," Ishmael announced. Yardena's eyes widened at the sight of the old man, and she shrank a bit into Hagar's arms. Abraham looked at the girl and then at Hagar. He opened his mouth to speak, but he caught Hagar's slight shake of her head and narrowing of her eyes. He understood.

"Can you talk to us?" Hagar asked. "Can you tell us what happened, please? Is Lot alive?"

In a small, quavering voice, Yardena began to tell the three of them what had happened to her master, Lot, and his family.

"Y...yes," she said as the tears again welled in her young eyes.

"Good, good, Yardena," Hagar said, looking up at Abraham as he silently sighed relief.

With continued prompting by Hagar and supportive nods by the other three, she related the story of the visit by the two strangers and the party that her mistress Ado gave for them. When she reached the part about the commotion in the street, Hagar and Abraham looked at each other, puzzled.

"What do you mean, 'There was a loud noise,' Yardena?" Hagar asked. "Who made the loud noise?"

"Men. From the city. They wanted to see the visitors. But my master Lot wouldn't let them. Then, the visitors made all of the men blind." Again, Yardena took a moment to screw up her little face and cry; the pain of the screaming sounds remained fresh in her head.

At this, Abraham and Hagar swapped knowing looks. Hagar shook her head in sadness.

Yardena composed herself a bit and continued.

"Then, my master Lot told me to help my mistress Ado prepare to leave. The strangers told us that they would destroy the city. So, I packed what I thought my mistress might need. Near dawn, the visitors took us out of the city and towards the river."

Abraham sighed, this time audibly. Yardena paused and looked up at him, thinking he wanted to ask something. He smiled warmly at her and came down on his knees in front of her, turning her to him fully and gently grasping her by the shoulders . They were almost eye to eye. Abraham couldn't stop himself from speaking.

"My child, you are a good girl to care for your master and mistress so. Please, tell us what happened then." This action reassured Yardena, Hagar saw, and now it was her turn to sigh a moment and offer a small prayer.

Once we were out of the city, one of the visitors told us, "Escape for your life. Do not look back or stop anywhere in the valley. Make your way to the hills."

Abraham gently brushed the girl's cheek with the back of his hand. "You're doing so well, my child," he said. "Go on."

"And then, my master Lot said to them, 'Oh, no, my lords, please let us go to the town of Zoar, not the hills.'"

Abraham glanced quizzically over the girl's shoulder towards Hagar. She shrugged. What Lot asked made no sense to her, either.

Yardena didn't notice this and continued. "One of the visitors told my master that he could go to Zoar and that the town would not be destroyed, but we should get there quickly because the Lord couldn't destroy the cities until we were safe."

"Good, good," said Abraham, nodding at Yardena, the relief showing on his face.

"By the time we reached Zoar, the sun was up in the east. Then…" Yardena paused at this and took a large breath in and out. "Then, we saw the fire falling from the sky…" She trailed off and sobbed again.

Abraham nodded and stood. He knew the rest. He reached down and touched the chin of the girl and raised her head to look at him. "Thank you, my child. You are a brave girl to come and tell us this."

Yardena held her hands up. "Oh, no, my lord, there is more," she said with no enthusiasm.

"Oh? Tell us, then, please."

"Almost the moment we came inside the gates of Zoar, we started to see the fire and the smoke coming from the sky in great sheets all down the valley of the river. The wind blew the smell of the smoke into our faces even though we were safe from the fire in the town."

"That's when my mistress Ado suddenly jumped up and ran through the gates of the town. No one moved to stop her because she ran without any word. I jumped up and followed her, calling to her to please wait for me because I wanted to help her if she needed anything. She was running back towards Sodom, the way we came. I don't know why. I don't know why."

The girl put her chin on her chest and took another long inhale and exhale. She seemed to be steeling herself for what she would say next.

In this pause, Abraham looked up at Hagar and realized that his own eyes were probably as wide with amazement as Hagar's were. Catching his look, Hagar slowly shook her head at Abraham with incredulity.

Yardena continued.

"I ran as fast as I could but my mistress," she swallowed hard, "ran faster. That's when…that's when it happened."

"What?" Abraham asked sharply. "What happened then?"

Yardena bit her bottom lip in an effort to not cry at the memory. "That's when I saw ahead of me … that some of the fire from the sky came down and struck my mistress Ado. I watched her… I watched her…" The girl could not keep back her tears any longer; they came out of her in a great flood.

Almost to himself, Abraham finished Yardena's thought for her. "You watched her die."

Yardena cried even louder as Abraham spoke the words. Hagar and Bracha ran to her and shushed her and soothed her.

Abraham asked, his own eyes wet with sadness, "And my nephew is still alive?" Yardena, through her tears, nodded.

"Bracha, why don't you take Yardena and Ishmael and feed them their breakfast," Hagar said. Bracha herded the children over to the side of the tent where she had been preparing the food. Hagar said to Abraham, "My lord, may we step outside?"

The pair of them stood outside the tent for a moment in silence, each one lost in thought. Finally, Abraham said, "I will send to Zoar to see about my nephew and his daughters, to see if there's anything they need."

Hagar agreed. "Yes, I think that is wise. And your nephew's daughters are of age and perhaps they can be a solace to their father in this terrible time."

"I wonder what Ado was thinking?" Abraham wondered aloud.

Hagar thought a moment and said, "I think I know. She did not want to leave behind the life that she had come to know and enjoy in Sodom. My heart tells me she went back for that. I know what it is like to leave a life behind, my lord."

"Yes, true," Abraham agreed, and he added, "But you learned that you should be where El put you. Ado never realized that."

Hagar considered this. "Yes, perhaps you're right."

The pair looked at each other sharing in the moment a great sadness for the family of Abraham's nephew. Finally, Hagar spoke. "What will you to do about Yardena?"

"I don't know. I don't think it would be wise to send her back to Lot. Her mother died having her, and her father is one of the herdsmen. I don't think there are any other relatives here."

Hagar had an idea. "My lord, perhaps she could be a helper to the wife of Eliezer. I know she has some sickness. Yardena could become like a granddaughter to the woman, and it would give the child a home and security."

"Hm. I had not considered that. You know, Hagar, you would perhaps make a shrewd manager of my affairs also," Abraham said, allowing himself a small smile.

It was Hagar's turn to smile slightly. "I am here to serve you, my lord."

The next day, Abraham dispatched three servants, a cart of olive oil, wine, and other foodstuffs to Zoar to find Lot and help him any way they could. Within the week, the men, the carts, and the supplies returned. Abraham, slightly irritated, ran out when he saw the filled carts and asked one of the men as they began to get down from the wagons, "Wait. Why didn't you give these things to my nephew? Is he not well?"

"My lord," the oldest one said, "we could not find him. We inquired at the town of Zoar, as you told us, and the people there said that, shortly after he arrived, your nephew and his daughters fled into the caves in the hills. We searched for them the best we could, but we did not find them. We were told, my lord, that your nephew has taken to drink."

His frustration turning to sadness, Abraham thanked the men and ordered that the contents of the carts be distributed among all of his servants.

Hagar never heard from Lot again. Within a few months, rumors came to Abraham's camp of the children that Lot's daughters bore, but no one would say out loud precisely who the fathers of the children were.

SIX

braham never told Hagar why he decided to leave their long-time home near Mamre's Oaks and move his ever-growing herds and servants and tents southward. She suspected that the loss of Lot, even if he had been somewhat of a thorn in Abraham's side for decades, still hurt the old man deeply. Abraham was nearly 100 years old, and being near the place where so much destruction had recently occurred may simply have been too much for him to bear.

So, after more than a decade, the entire camp became nomads again and picked up and moved to Gerar, between Kadesh and Shur, along the route towards Egypt. Everyone was told that Gerar boasted good grazing land and adequate water. While the compound began packing for the move, Eliezer and Abraham journeyed ahead of the group and negotiated water rights with the king, one Abimelech. Sarah and her servant accompanied them to the meeting with the king. Word was sent back that the talks with the king were successful. So, there seemed little reason not to move the flocks and people to Gerar. Yet, almost to a person, each one in the camp expressed regret that they were leaving the large, shady oak trees of Mamre's land.

Abraham took the move as a reason to remove Ishmael from Hagar's tent. "I should have had the boy come live with me sooner," he told her. "A boy his age should be with the men by now."

"He helps you in the fields already, my lord," she said in an attempt to make Abraham think that this was enough of a concession.

"True, but he is too old to be with women all the time. He is nearly thirteen now. When we move to Gerar, he will come live in my tent."

"As you wish, my lord," Hagar's mouth said calmly, but her heart screamed in pain.

And other news came as well. It was immediately before the move that Sarah announced the news that she was with child. Once the group had made their settlement at Gerar, Abraham held a feast to mark the announcement. Hagar, not wanting to seem petty or jealous, attended, but she kept silent throughout the event. Eliezer, Abraham, and some of the other men made small speeches praising El for the blessing. During Abraham's turn to talk, Sarah looked at Hagar sitting across the circle from her and gave Hagar a self-satisfied smile. Hagar returned this look with a slight nodding bow as she sat. She thought, "Never let it be said to Abraham by anyone that I showed Sarah anything but respect."

One morning soon after the feast, a group of shouting riders appeared in the camp after the men had left to the fields for the day. They announced that they were soldiers from Gerar, the guard of

King Abimelech. Hagar and the other women of Abraham's group came out of their tents or left their work to see what the commotion was about. One soldier, brandishing a short, thick sword that he whirled threateningly around his head, loudly demanded to know where he could find Abraham. An older woman nearby told the soldiers that Abraham and the men were in the pastures and had taken the flocks to water there. The loud soldier then asked which tent was Sarah's. Again, the old woman told him, and pointed to it.

The riders galloped their horses to Sarah's tent; two of them went inside. The women in the compound could hear Sarah's voice yelling at the men. A crash of plates and jugs was heard. Then, Sarah screamed. The two men brought her out, each one carrying her by an arm, and put her on one of the donkeys with a rider behind her. Sarah screamed threats to the men as they did so, telling them that Abraham would see them quartered for what they were doing to her. The other women covered their faces with fear; many ran back into their tents. Hagar, watching this scene from the other end of the compound, knew that Abraham must be told about this immediately.

As the group of riders disappeared towards Gerar with Sarah, Hagar ran back into her tent and told Bracha, "Go! Find Abraham! Bring him here! They've taken Sarah!" Bracha immediately stood and dropped the sewing she had been working on and ran out the back of the tent to find Abraham.

Soon, the old man ran breathlessly into Hagar's tent with Eliezer and Bracha close at his heels. "What? What happened to my wife?" he cried. To Hagar, he seemed almost close to panic. He pulled nervously at his chin as he spoke.

"My lord, men from the king of Gerar came and took Sarah away."

"Did they harm her?" he asked, his eyes wide with worry and fear.

"I don't think so, my lord." Hagar thought it wise to not tell about the struggle that Sarah offered.

"Abimelech," Eliezer said to Abraham from behind him. "It is about the water."

Abraham turned and nodded to his man, his voice and breathing starting to return to normal, "Ah, I understand now."

"Understand what, my lord?" Hagar asked confusedly.

He turned back to Hagar. "In exchange for letting our flocks water at his wells and streams, I promised to provide Abimelech a wife." Looking back at Eliezer, he added, "He thinks she is my sister."

"Probably," the man answered.

"And not my wife."

"Probably," he said again, nodding. "You told him as much when you first spoke, my lord."

"Yes, yes." Abraham winced as he replied as if the memory of what he said to Abimelech pained him.

"Like Merikare," Eliezer reminded him.

"Yes, I know. Thank you, Eliezer," Abraham said, a trace of agitation in his voice.

Hagar had never before heard Abraham mention the confusion surrounding the way she came to be with him and Sarah. She knew the story; she had heard the details of it from Eliezer soon after she had been given to Sarah as a servant. But to hear Abraham speak of it brought back images of her life in Egypt. She felt compelled to speak.

"My lord, surely God-Who-Sees-Me will protect my mistress Sarah. He will protect you and her like he did with..." she paused and swallowed, the thought of the situation so many years ago again fresh in her mind, "Merikare."

Abraham turned to Hagar. "I pray it is so, Hagar. I pray so."

Eliezer, always the pragmatist, brought Abraham back to the realities of the situation. "My lord, what are we to do about this?" he asked.

"It is delicate," Abraham noted. "We cannot afford to offend the king and have him deny us water rights. And," he added with a sigh, "I did promise him a wife."

"But, surely, my lord, you don't mean to let the king keep your wife, Sarah?" Hagar asked incredulously. "What about the child she carries?"

"Of course not; I have no intention of letting him keep her. Yet, I cannot simply go to Abimelech and demand that he return her to me, child or no."

"No. You are right."

"I think we do nothing for the moment. We must rely on El to remedy the situation. Hagar, you said it well yourself," Abraham said with finality.

The next morning, the soldiers from Abimelech returned to the camp. Abraham, who had spent the night sleeplessly appealing to El for help, sat in front of his tent as was often his custom in the early mornings. He leapt to his feet when the riders came into the compound.

"Abraham!" they shouted to no one in particular as they rode in a circle around the compound. Fingers and hands pointed to the old man standing at the tent door. The riders turned their animals in his direction and pulled up in front of him.

"King Abimelech orders you to come to his house, now."

From the front opening of their tent, Hagar and Bracha came out to watch the scene, and they heard the command the men gave Abraham. Ishmael, who was coming by his mother's tent for some of Bracha's breakfast cakes, also saw what was happening and asked, some fear registering in his voice, "What do the men want with father?"

Rather than a sense of dread, however, Hagar knew in her heart that God-Who-Sees-Me had indeed protected Sarah and Abraham. With a smile, Hagar said, "It is nothing, my son. How are you?" She tapped Ishmael on the shoulder to take his attention away from the scene, and they returned inside for their morning meal as Abraham and Eliezer made ready to go to Abimelech with the soldiers. "Come, my son, Bracha has made your favorites; all will be well. I promise," she reassured him.

That evening, as Abraham and Eliezer returned joyously to the camp with Sarah, the word that went around the compound was that all had happened as Hagar said it would. It seemed that El had come to Abimelech in a dream the night before and had threatened the king and his entire family if he did not return Sarah to Abraham immediately. The dream was so real and so threatening to Abimelech that, when he rose before dawn, he immediately ordered Abraham to him so he could return Sarah and to ask why Abraham did not tell him that Sarah was his wife.

Apparently, the threats made by El to the king during the night motivated him to give Abraham even more; not only did he return Sarah, but he also sent several of his servants, foodstuffs, animals, and a large quantity of silver from his city's coffers. "Pray to your God for me," he begged Abraham, according to what Eliezer told her later.

The water rights were never an issue again, and no wife was ever given to Abimelech.

SEVEN

Sarah seemed to suffer no ill effects from her night in Abimelech's house. She carried the baby to the full term and had a male child a year almost to the day from the time the visitors from El said she would.

Abraham told anyone who would listen how marvelous El's blessings to him had been. He constantly praised El for the wondrous miracle of giving him not only one but now two sons, and one of them by his 90-year-old wife!

And, as the messengers told her to, Sarah named the baby boy Isaac. As many of the women crowded around Sarah when she brought him out to be seen in public for the first time, Sarah slightly changed the story of the reason for the name. Hagar, standing on the edge of the crowd of women, noted that Sarah said she chose the name Isaac because of her great joy in giving Abraham a son at such an old age—it had made her laugh, so, the boy's name was to be Isaac. Sarah mentioned nothing about that laugh having been a bitter and cynical one, made a year earlier at the tent door when El's messengers prophesied about the birth of the boy.

Abraham held a great feast to mark the circumcision of Isaac on the eighth day after his birth. He invited many of Gerar's wealthiest citizens to join him in the celebration. Abimelech, even though invited, decided not to attend. Hagar and Ishmael, however, were happy to go and enjoy the moment. "We are happy for our master Abraham and our mistress Sarah, aren't we?" she said to her son as he came to get her from her tent and to escort her to their places around the great circle.

Great plates of meat and fruits and breads carried by servants made their way around the circle of celebrants. Not too far from where they sat, Hagar spied Yardena as she served Eliezer's wife, and the girl saw her, too. Hagar nudged her son and said, "There's your friend," and pointed to Yardena. The boy and girl exchanged quick waves and smiles. It was an evening for happiness in the camp, it seemed.

Sarah certainly seemed happy, Hagar thought. She laughed more that night than Hagar believed she had heard her laugh in the decade in her service, sharing her tent. Her beaming, proud smile could easily be seen from across the circle of celebrants and well-wishers. Abraham, sitting at her side, seemed equally as pleased.

After the filling meal, musicians and dancers entertained the full and happy crowd. Ishmael sat quietly during the feast, watching people come and go to Sarah and the baby for a look. Finally, as if making up his mind, Ishmael asked his mother, "May I go see Isaac?"

Hagar considered this for a moment. "Go to our mistress Sarah. Ask her if you may. If she says you cannot see him, do not argue with her."

"Yes, mother."

Ishmael almost tiptoed around behind Sarah as she cradled Isaac in her arms. One of the Gerarites had just then walked away after admiring the baby boy when Ishmael spoke to her softly.

"Mistress Sarah? May I please see your baby?"

Sarah turned around, a bit startled that a voice came from behind her. When she saw that the speaker was Ishmael, her mouth turned down for the first time all evening. "What do you want," she asked sharply.

"I...I wish to see my brother," the boy said meekly.

Abraham heard, turned, and saw the situation. "Of course you may, my son!" He said. He reached out to take Isaac from Sarah to let Ishmael have a good look. She pulled away from her husband and uttered a low, almost hissing sound.

"No! I will show him my child!" she snapped. Sarah roughly held out her infant son to Ishamel. "There! Is that what you wanted? Well?" she demanded.

Abraham's face bore a dismayed look. "There is no need for that..." he said and shook his head. "Let the boy see his brother."

Ishmael smiled weakly at the child. "He's...he's a fine boy," he said.

Sarah pulled her son back to her breast, looked down at him and said, "He'll be a finer man than you will ever be."

Abraham's mouth flew open. "Sarah!" he said in an almost scolding tone.

Hagar watched the scene with great interest from the far side of the circle. She saw Sarah's motions and sour mouth and knew that the meeting had not gone well. She saw Ishmael suddenly bow slightly to both his father and to Sarah and make his way back towards her. She then saw Abraham lean over to Sarah and speak to her, his hand gesturing violently as he spoke. Hagar knew that Abraham was gently scolding his other wife.

Several of the guests pointed towards Abraham and Sarah and leaned their heads together to speak. Some pointed at Hagar as they whispered.

Hagar turned behind her to Bracha, who had also been helping serve that evening. Bracha, too, had seen what had happened, and, even though neither one had heard the words of the exchange between Sarah and Ishmael, they both understood the meaning. Bracha's face was red with anger towards Sarah and with hurt for Ishmael.

When the boy reached his mother's side again, his face was flushed as well. Hagar decided to downplay the event for her son's and Abraham's sake and pretend nothing had happened.

"Is everything well? So, what did you think of your brother?"

Ishmael remained quiet for a moment after sitting back down. "He is smaller than I thought he would be," he said sadly.

His mother laughed a bit. "He will probably always be smaller than you, my son," Hagar said, trying to make him feel better. "That is why he is your little brother."

Ishmael looked up and rewarded his mother with the smile she teased out of him.

Life among Abraham's group then settled back into the daily routine. Hagar never quite grew accustomed to having Ishmael live with his father. Many times during the evenings she would have a thought and turn to share it with Ishmael, only to realize that he no longer lived with her.

Over the course of the next two years, Ishmael stopped by his mother's tent less and less frequently. He came when he could, but most of the time he could be found in the company of Abraham. Where father went, son went also. It delighted Abraham that Ishmael took such an interest in his work and showed great aptitude in managing both men and flocks.

One evening after his work in the fields had ended, Ishmael ran into Hagar's tent with a fistful of meadow flowers. He threw them at his mother and said, "For you, my mother!" and ran out. She hadn't had time to speak to him before he was off. It struck Hagar suddenly that her son's voice was changing, he was a bit taller than she, and he was beginning to show dark hair on his chin and under his nose. "Our little boy has grown up," she said, looking at the flowers strewn on the cushions about her. Bracha smiled warmly and nodded.

Sarah—who had always remained inside her tent during the days to stay cool and to not have to see or speak to many servants— suddenly could be seen walking throughout the camp with Isaac on her shoulder or strapped to her side. It was as if her pride had been completely focused onto this child; Hagar could understand that. Hagar was also surprised to learn that Sarah had chosen to nurse the boy herself; that, too, was a miracle of El.

As the child grew, his face showed that he definitely was Abraham's son. Even at that early age, the nose was unmistakable. And Isaac began walking early. Soon, he often toddled out of Sarah's tent and would wobble around the center of the compound, chased by Sarah and the servant girl, all three of them laughing. Hagar felt happiness in her heart for Sarah, even with all the bitterness between them. Their game of chase put Hagar in mind of the joyous times she had spent on the river with her mother all those years ago.

Then, one day, word spread around the camp that the time had come for the party marking Isaac's weaning and the first cutting of his hair.

EIGHT

S arah insisted that the celebration for Isaac be much larger than any feast that Abraham had produced so far. She spent days in the marketplace at Gerar, searching for the best wines and olives and dates and spices. She sent out invitations to all the neighboring kingdoms and even reached out to some of the people who lived in the area of the Oaks of Mamre, telling them to come and celebrate and reunite.

She also insisted that there be double the usual musicians and performers. No expense would be spared for her son, she said loudly and often, as she made her way around the camp. Abraham didn't argue. A few times he raised his eyebrows at her requests but he never told her, "No."

Additionally, Sarah ordered that the celebration continue over two days. Abraham finally contested this, but Sara won him over with little effort. It was easier for Abraham to give her what she wanted than to listen to her complain. Besides, Abraham, too, wanted to celebrate Isaac, and was happy that Sarah was so excited about the child, so he allowed her a great deal of leeway.

Sarah also decided to make the first day of the feast center around the ceremony of the cutting of the hair. The second day would see most of the entertainment—the dancers she had hired and the musicians that she had brought in from far and wide—and would also be the the day for visiting with the out-of-town guests.

Hagar, wanting to help if she could, sent word through Sara's servant girl that she would make Bracha available to assist with the preparations if needed. The servant girl returned to Hagar with a curt answer from Sarah: "Never."

Hagar could not understand Sarah's constant anger. Of course, even in her heart of hearts, Hagar still felt a sense of pride over who she was and where she was from, but she had let most of that go over the years. Those things seemed so much less important now compared to watching Ishmael grow, and enjoying the friendship of Bracha and, especially, being happy in the ongoing knowledge of God-Who-Sees-Me. It was a peace that Hagar enjoyed, but she knew that Sarah, somehow, never seemed to have that peace about her.

The first day of the feast seemed to go well. Everyone was in a good mood, and Isaac did not put up much of a fuss when his hair was cut, like so many other babies seemed to do. Sarah clapped and laughed, happy that her boy made such a good showing in front of all the visitors. The day concluded with not one, not two, but three large calves, the succulent meat roasted to perfection, brought in by several servants for the pleasure of the guests, who washed down the meal with some good wine.

As everyone made their way to bed, satisfied and happy, Sarah, her face still flushed with joy and a little wine, loudly reminded the crowd, "And just think! We're going to do this celebrating all over again tomorrow!"

Hagar and Bracha, tired from the day's revelry, found their beds quickly. Ishmael stuck his head through the tent flap as the women were settling down and said, "Good night, mother. Good night Bracha. I will see you both tomorrow."

"Wait, my so…" Hagar began, rising from her cushions in the darkness.

He was gone before she had the chance to wish him good night in return.

The party resumed near midday. This second day, however, began with the different musicians who took their turns before the center of the circle where the fire pit was; everyone clapped in time to the music and seemed to appreciate the talents of the groups who performed. The happy mood from the day before continued. Abraham and Sarah, with Isaac between them on his own cushions, watched and beamed with pleasure.

More food came and even more food after that. Wine, too, flowed freely. As the afternoon wore on, the dancers came to entertain; young men who performed amazing leaps and flips and contortions amazed and delighted the crowd. Then, the women dancers started their routines to great applause.

By early evening, with the wine taking hold of many in the audience and with the center fire lit, some of the dancers found that celebrants from the crowd jumped up and joined their circles. No one seemed to mind. Abraham and Sarah laughed and applauded as friends and neighbors all joined in the celebratory dancing, linking their hands with the dancers, the circle growing wider and wider around the center fire. One dancer from Gerar, an older woman, broke off from the chain, came up to Abraham and said, "My lord, won't you join us?" Abraham laughed and clapped, but the dancer persisted. "Yes, come, sir, join us!" Abraham waved her off, and the woman shrugged. She turned to Sarah.

"Mistress? Won't you dance with us?" She held her hand out to help Sarah rise. Sarah looked at Abraham and said, "Oh, it has been years since I have danced, my husband! I think I will!" She bent and gave a kiss to Isaac and leapt to her feet, the crowd roaring in laughter and approval as she took the dancer's hand and began to circle with the others.

No one, not even Abraham, seemed to notice that Isaac had gotten up and tottered after his mother.

Except for Ishmael.

From the other side of the circle, the young man, who had been enjoying the dancing as much as everyone else, suddenly narrowed his eyes as he saw his young brother move side to side towards the dancers in search of his mother. The drunken dancers, the music, and darkness and shadows all raced through his mind as dangers to the boy. He jumped up and ran to the circle. Hagar thought he was joining the dance. "Yes!" she said approvingly, "Go enjoy yourself, my son!"

But Ishmael didn't hear her. He quickly made his way to the other side of the circle. As he approached his brother, a drunken dancer stumbled out of the group and close to the boy. Ishmael roughly pushed the man aside and scooped up his brother in his arms, almost in the same motion. The action caused Isaac to open his mouth and eyes in surprise. His little face and long nose crinkled suddenly into tears with fright at being in the arms of his brother. Ishmael, taken aback a moment by this reaction, began to laugh.

"Oh, my little man! All is well! It is I, your brother, Ishmael! You must be careful!"

Isaac screamed in fright, turning around and squirming in his brother's arms, searching for the mother he thought he had lost. It was at that moment that Sarah's screams brought the music and dancing to an abrupt halt.

Somehow, above the din, she had heard her son's cries. "You!" Sarah screamed, as if she had been stabbed in her heart. "You! Put down my son!" The circle of dancers stopped as if frozen and parted as a wave in the sea to turn and see what caused her to yell so.

Ishmael's mouth flew open in protest. "Mistress, I was...," he began, but Sarah cut him off.

"I said for you to put my son down! How dare you make him cry! And to laugh at him! I saw you!"

No one seemed to know what to do. The entire party looked on as if the exchange were a performance. Abraham stood immediately when he heard his wife's anguished cries, knocking a plate of food from his own lap. Yet, he, too, could only watch.

Hagar also stood, but her standing was out of fear, not anger or surprise.

Sarah moved quickly towards the two boys. Isaac, seeing his mother, reached out for her from Ishmael's arms. She snatched her son away from Ishmael, who held out his hands in innocent protest.

Sarah turned viciously towards Abraham on the outside of the circle, spit flying from the corners of her mouth as she continued angrily. "And you! I have told you before. Get rid of that slave woman and her son! Don't you see? When you die, she and that boy," she pointed behind her with a long, accusatory finger at Ishmael, "will get all that you have. I want my son to be your heir. Not hers."

In the moment of silence that followed, the crackle of the fire and a stirring of some of the tent flaps in the breeze were all that could be heard.

Hagar's blood suddenly ran cold. She saw how angry Sarah had become. It put her in mind of the night she was beaten by the older woman. Except this time, there was more hatred in her voice than ever before.

Abraham finally found his own voice. "My wife," he said, clearing his throat, "we must speak of this later."

Yet, Sarah was not to be put off. "No! We will speak of it now!" Sarah insisted.

She turned in the circle, her son now only whimpering since he had found his mother's arms, and found Hagar standing in the light of one of the torches that surrounded the circle. "I suspect you put him up to this!" she said, moving her head in the direction of Ishmael.

All that was within Hagar wanted to scream back at Sarah, but she only bowed her head. She knew what was coming. "God-Who-Sees-Me," she prayed as Sarah continued to pelt her with insults and accusations, "help me keep my tongue."

"And you have always tried to take my place with my husband," Sarah said, still spitting with anger. She wheeled around to attack Abraham. "And you have encouraged her!"

Abraham, clearly embarrassed, tried to establish some authority over his wife. "My Sarah, you must listen to me. Stop this madness." He moved towards her and the baby.

She stopped him by stepping back quickly from his advance and uttering something akin to a growl, almost as a dog protecting her pup.

The crowd had begun to slowly back away from the circle and silently disappear into the night, the emotions of the moment quickly sobering most of them. The musicians and dancers began quietly to gather their things and go to their tents and homes. The feast was clearly over in light of Sarah's outbursts. In her tantrum, Sarah hardly seemed to notice or care.

"You must choose this night! Do you want her," Sarah said, her voice emphasizing the last word, "or me? Either she goes, or my son and I go."

"There it is," Hagar thought; she knew it was no idle threat. Now, with the birth of Isaac, the sword has been drawn and thrust into the heart of Abraham.

Sarah now wept, the emotions of over ten years of having to see Hagar as a wife and mother every day in front of her and the entire camp proving to be too much to hold back any longer. She had her son and now demanded that he be made sole heir.

Hagar never doubted which way Abraham would choose.

Abraham moved closer to the center of the circle, but this time Sarah held her ground and only moved Isaac closer to her chest. The boy now seemed content at his mother's embrace and had stopped his crying. Abraham looked at Sarah and Isaac; then he looked at Ishmael, still standing with his open hands in mute protest. Abraham then looked across the circle to where Hagar stood with her head bowed.

"I...I cannot send them out, my wife. He is my son. I have made her my wife. You know this. But you also know that no one can replace you in my heart. Ever."

Sarah would not be satisfied. She shook her head slowly from side to side.

"You must choose. We will wait for your answer," she said defiantly, and she took her son past Abraham and headed to her tent. Abraham tried to reach out to her as she passed, but Sarah side-stepped his hand and continued onward.

That left Hagar and Ishmael alone with Abraham. For a moment, none of the three spoke.

Then, the vacuum in the tension caused by Sarah's departure moved Ishmael into speech. "Mother! Father! I did nothing to the boy! I only saw that he was walking in the paths of the dancers. I only wanted to protect him!"

Abraham shushed him with a head shake. "Rest, my son. I know you meant no harm. You were trying to help. It does not matter. There was nothing you did or did not do. This is not about you."

"No," Hagar agreed, lifting her voice and head to speak to Abraham. "This goes back much farther than you, Ishmael."

"She is serious this time," Hagar added.

"Yes, I can see that."

"You know what must happen, do you not?"

Abraham's eyes began to tear, and he turned to Ishmael. The old man considered for a moment then said, "No. I cannot. I simply cannot."

"You must," Hagar said calmly. "You have no choice. She is not only your wife. She is also your sister."

"No. No. No."

"Oh, my blessed, good lord, you who have been so good to me, to us. You cannot help that you love her as you do."

Abraham brought both fists to his eyes as if he could wipe away the events of the evening.

"No, you are correct. I cannot help it. I have always loved her. I always shall do so."

"And you are forgetting something. God-Who-Sees-Me is with us."

Ishmael began to realize the situation. He who had been loved by almost everyone his whole life—it had never crossed his mind that such a thing were even possible.

"Father! No! Mother!" He ran to her side, but Hagar still looked only at Abraham.

"What are you saying? We...we cannot leave. Mistress Sarah will become calm. She always does. Look, I will apologize..."

"No, my son," Hagar said, still looking at Abraham. "You heard us. This time, it does not matter. Nothing will calm her. Isaac has changed everything." She paused.

"Hasn't he, my lord?"

Abraham brought his hands away from his face. His watery eyes grew wide with sadness.

"Yes."

"Then...I hate him!" Ishmael said, bursting into tears. "I will kill him!" he added with a sob.

Hagar turned to her son. "Oh, no, my son. No. Do not let hate consume you. It leads to no good. Revenge will destroy you instead." She reached out and hugged him. The young man buried his face in her shoulder and cried.

"I'm sorry, mother. I'm so sorry. I could never hurt him."

"I know, my son. I know. All will be well. Hush, now." She noticed for the first time that Ishmael had to stoop slightly in her embrace. The realization made her smile for a moment.

Abraham came over quickly and placed his hands on them both in blessing. Hagar's smile grew warmer as she looked at him. Her own eyes, too, began to tear.

From his mother's shoulder, Ishmael looked up at his father. "Father…please. No. Please," he sobbed.

Abraham said nothing for a moment. He looked from mother to son and back again. "I will make you both a promise. I will go to El for guidance. This I promise."

"I think you should," Hagar said. "And I think Ishmael should stay with us tonight, if you agree, my lord."

He removed his hands from them. "Yes. Yes. Perhaps that is wise. I wish you both a good night." He turned and made his way into the darkness beyond the circle.

"Let us go, my boy," Hagar said. Then, correcting herself, she added with a sad smile, "My young man." The pair turned from the circle as well, and saw that Bracha stood on the edge of the firelight behind them. Her face was flush with anger and frustration.

"Bracha!" Hagar said. "Did you hear all of what was said?" Hagar needed no answer. She could clearly see from the set jaw and firm gaze of Bracha that the young woman seethed with anger. Bracha's nostrils practically flared with bitterness.

"Then you heard what I said to Ishmael," Hagar reminded her. "Anger and revenge will not do any of us any good now." She took Bracha by her free arm and turned her towards their tent. "We must wait until Abraham decides what to do. I feel sure I know what his choice will be."

"He can't send us away, can he, mother?"

As they entered the darkness towards Hagar's tent, she answered Ishmael's question by saying, "Bracha, I want you to go to the other tents and get what bags you can."

She added, "We must pack."

After Abraham left the circle, he walked outside of the camp for some distance. Sarah's words and anger still rang in his ears, as did Hagar's calmness and Ishmael's pleadings. He could not imagine life without his beloved son, Ishmael. And, he had come to care deeply for Hagar. But he knew she was right; Sarah was not to be put off this time. He knew of her jealousy. Everyone did. He thought at first that the birth of Isaac would soothe her some. In some ways it had. But the depth of her anger and hurt—no, he now understood that Isaac had become only another issue of competition between the two women, at least in Sarah's mind. And he did not realize that until tonight.

Abraham reached a knoll above the camp. He turned back towards it and looked down at it and thought of the lives of all the servants and friends and family below him. He held his hands towards the stars and said, "Oh, El, God of Gods, God of the promise, I thank You for all You have given me. I thank you for my health. My wealth. My servants. My wives." He paused a moment. "My sons."

The hillside suddenly became swirled with the wind that always seemed to accompany the presence of El. The voice said, "Abraham. You are troubled."

"Yes, my Lord. I do not want to lose my son. But I do not want to lose my Sarah."

"Do not worry about Ishmael and Hagar, Abraham. He is a child of the promise, remember. I will bless him and make him mighty. But Sarah's son is the one who will fulfill the promise of the blessing I gave you. Do not doubt that, either."

"I do not doubt you, El, my Lord. But Lord, I fear for them if they go."

"I know you do, Abraham. I know. Trust me. Hagar is my beloved as well. I will protect them."

Abraham looked down at the camp. "Yes. I trust. Help me to trust You more."

The wind swirled again briefly and then, as quickly as it came, it subsided.

Abraham had his answer and made his way back to the camp.

The first hint of light in the east broke through the night when Abraham came to Hagar's tent. What greeted him when he entered took him by surprise. Hagar and Ishmael sat cross-legged on a carpet in the center facing the front. They greeted Abraham with grim looks. Ishmael seemed to be trying to avoid his father's eyes, but Hagar bowed her head slightly when Abraham looked at her. Around and behind them were bags of their belongings. Bracha could be seen in the back of the tent, tying string around another bundle of clothing.

"What are you doing? What have you done?"

Hagar paused, then she smiled weakly. "My lord, we know what you have decided. God-Who-Sees-Me is also the God-Who-Hears, remember?" And she touched the hand of her son as she said so.

"Ah," Abraham said, the tears starting again in his aged eyes. "I might have guessed that you already knew."

"I think I knew when I returned from the desert the first time," she said, her smile spreading slightly. "Before this young man here was even born. I knew it would come to this."

"I never thought it would."

"It has," Hagar sighed.

Bracha, finished with the last bundle, came up and tossed it on the pile with the rest. She made no attempt at hiding her anger toward Abraham, going so far as to glare at him before Hagar shook her head at her. The young woman stormed off to the back of the tent once again.

"She is frightened more than angry," Hagar explained.

"I understand." Then, "I have animals waiting for you when you are ready to go. And food and water."

"We are ready. We have been ready," Hagar said flatly.

"Yes. I see that. Anything you need?"

"My lord, would you please allow Bracha to go with us?"

"Of course," he answered. "I never thought otherwise."

Hagar looked towards the back of the tent and met Bracha's shining blue eyes. They exchanged small smiles.

"Then, that is all we need, my lord."

Mother and son rose from their sitting positions, and Ishmael, overcome with emotion, ran to his father and grabbed him about the waist in a hug. His silent tears mirrored Abraham's. The two of them walked outside the tent, and Hagar and Bracha followed. Five donkeys waited there along with some of the young servants.

"Go inside and get their baggage," Abraham ordered, and the young men did so, bringing two or three bags in each hand and tying them to two of the animals.

Ishmael still clung to his father's waist. Abraham took Ishmael's hands from around him and looked at them in his own. "My son..." he began, choking up as he realized that it was the last time he would use those words to Ishmael. "Help your mother and Bracha get on their animals," he said, patting Ishmael on the cheek.

"Yes, father." Ishmael obeyed, assisting the women and then mounting his own donkey.

"You have water and food. Here is a bag of silver. It will get you on your way."

"Yes. We will manage. Thank you."

The early morning sun was beginning to brighten the sky, and Eliezer ran up at that moment. "Hagar!" he said, his voice showing more emotion than Hagar had previously heard in it. "I wanted to wish you all farewell. I know El will guide you and protect you."

"Yes. He will, good sir. I thank you for your kindness to us all these years."

Eliezer bowed low before the three of them. "The honor has been mine, my mistress."

Hagar nodded in gratitude and approval. It was the first time any of the household had called her such.

"Where will you go, Hagar?" Eliezer asked.

"Towards Egypt. It is all that I know now."

"Blessings."

"To you and yours, also. Greet Yardena for us."

"I shall," he said, stepping back.

Looking across the compound, Hagar thought she saw the flap of Sarah's tent close, but she did not care if the woman saw them or not.

Abraham then stepped forward. Overcome with emotion, he grabbed Hagar's hand and kissed it. She touched her heart with her free hand as he did so.

"Thank you, my child," he said.

"Goodbye, Abraham."

He stepped back and raised his hands to them in blessing. The three of them silently turned and rode southward. From their donkeys, Bracha and Ishmael each led one of the pack animals.

Hagar rode in front. Abraham kept his hands raised as long as he could see them. None of the three turned to see.

As the little group rode out of sight, Abraham realized that it was the first time Hagar had called him by name.

NINE

The water ran out sooner than Hagar thought it would. While still in the green area of Canaan, they had no trouble, but once they started on the road to Shur, water became scarce. Some of the watering holes had dried up and disappeared in the years since she had come that way, and travelers on the route were much fewer than she had anticipated. Not that they would be willing to part with their precious water.

Of course, the animals suffered first. She told the other two to dismount, that it would be easier on the donkeys if they all walked. Even that did not help after a time. One of the pack animals died first. Hagar knew that the other animals could not carry the extra load.

"We must get rid of some of our things," she said. "It will make our journey easier." Every time they stopped, they made a quick inventory of what they could afford to do without, each stop reducing what they carried until only the essentials remained.

Once, they saw in the distance some trees that promised a well.

"Mother!" Ishmael said, his young eyes seeing it first, "We are saved!" He dropped the lead of his animals and ran ahead. But once Hagar and Bracha reached the palms, they found Ishmael almost in tears. The water had become brackish and undrinkable. Still, the shade proved good, and Hagar said they would camp for the night and get an early start the next day.

Before dawn, Hagar wakened Bracha. "I will take Ishmael," she said, "we will get some of the empty water skins and find water. You stay here with the animals." Bracha shook her head, "No." Hagar knew she feared for them. "Yes, it will be only for a part of a day." Her talking caused Ishmael to wake. He listed to his mother continue. "We can cover more ground faster if it is only the two of us. No one will bother you here. The regular travelers already know this well is fouled." Bracha, still unconvinced, agreed.

"We will be back before sundown," Hagar promised as she and Ishmael took some water skins and walking sticks and headed southward.

By noon, two other wells had been found, but both of them had been filled in with debris. "Probably a war or a tribal dispute," Hagar said shrugging to Ishmael. "Let's press on."

"We won't make it back by sundown if we go on, mother," he answered.

Hagar squinted at the sun, her brown face wrinkled as she calculated the time. "No, but maybe if we go on and find something we will make it back not too much later." The two of them went on in silence. Other wells were found, but they, too, proved to be empty. One of them had buzzards circling it as they approached, and they found the bones of cattle nearby when they reached the well.

As the sun began to move westward, Ishmael again reminded

her mother that it was time to turn back, but his mother insisted that they continue to search. "The animals need water. We are almost out ourselves. Do you have any left in your skins?" Ishmael shook his head. "I have some but not much," Hagar told him. "We must find water soon, or we might not live, my son."

"But surely Bracha still has some with the animals. Let's go back to her."

Hagar turned to look behind them. She bit her lip in thought. "Where was the well that had the animal bones next to it?" she asked.

"Behind us to the west," Ishmael said after a moment to consider and turning to look in the direction his mother looked.

"Are you sure?" Hagar asked, shading her eyes with a brown hand and scanning the horizon behind them. She couldn't recall clearly.

"No. Wait. It was to the east. It was the one before the last one. Wasn't it?"

"I am not sure."

"Mother," Ishmael said, his voice cracking a bit in rising fear, "are we lost?"

"I…I am afraid so, my son. Let us try to rest some. We will rise when the sun is lower and it is cooler. Then we can find our way back."

Bracha will be so worried," he said.

"Yes," Hagar said. "Yes, she will be. But let us rest a bit."

They threw the water skins off their shoulders and dropped them on the grassless ground. Then, lying on them, the pair made small tents with their walking sticks, propping up the backs of their robes to create shade over their heads.

Hagar woke herself with a cry. It was dark and cold. She rolled over and shook Ishmael. He woke and said, "What is it, mother?"

"We have slept too long. We were more tired than I thought."

The two of them stood and shouldered the water bags in the darkness. The moonless night sky glittered with stars. "Do you have the skin with the water?" Hagar asked Ishmael. The young man turned away.

"I...I drank the last of it while you slept."

Hagar had no answer other than to say, "We must try to find our way back to Bracha. She must be mad with worry."

By morning, the early sun had turned the land almost instantly from cold to scorching hot. By noon, their lips had cracked with the lack of water. Hagar's tongue had swollen and her mouth was filled with the desert's dust. They had each thrown off the water skins and were practically staggering forward.

In the middle of the afternoon, Ishmael said, "Mother, I don't think I can go on." His voice was weak and thick with thirst.

"You must," she answered. "We must."

"Can't we stop again?"

"No."

She staggered on. After a moment, Hagar realized that Ishmael wasn't beside her. She turned and saw him stretched out on the sand behind her. She ran back to him as quickly as she could. He lay face up in the scorching sun, crying, but no tears came from his eyes.

"I can't mother. I can't. Leave me here."

"You must stand."

"I don't think so," he said almost dreamily.

Hagar looked around her desperately. She spied a small, brown scrub bush nearby. "Come, my son. I will help you. Let us rest under that bush." Ishmael struggled to his feet on the promise of rest under some shade. Hagar led him to the bush and said, "You stay here. I will come back for you."

Hagar could not bear to watch Ishmael suffer. Her heart broke as she left her son there. She knew he would die, and soon.

Walking some distance off, she, too, collapsed on the ground with exhaustion and thirst. "God-Who-Sees-Me, I need You now," she thought.

Then, a breeze stirred. Hagar closed her eyes and threw her head back to catch the coolness as the wind washed over her.

The voice said, "Hagar."

"Yes, my Lord."

"What is wrong?"

Her eyes still shut, Hagar thought, "What is right?"

The voice continued. "Don't be afraid. Go get your son. He will live and become a mighty nation. Do not forget my promises to you."

"Water…" she said, half in prayer and half in fear.

"Open your eyes, Hagar."

She did. She saw, just on the horizon to the west, palm trees— green palm trees.

"There is a well. Go to it. Get water. Save your son. I have heard your cries, and his. Have you forgotten?"

She shook her head. She would never forget.

He was God-Who-Sees-Me and God-Who-Hears.

EPILOGUE

The first of the dawn light created an eerie glow around the two brothers as they sat before the tent.

Isaac shook his head in amazement. "I can't believe I have never heard any of this before."

Ishmael nodded. "It is true. All of it."

"All?"

"Yes. All. We found Bracha—the animals had died by the time we returned—and brought her to the well that God had shown us. We then made our way to Egypt. We lived there for a time. My mother eventually found a suitable wife for me, the granddaughter of Tefibi, the slave buyer. She has been my wife ever since."

Again, Isaac could only shake his head in wonder. "That is like me and my Rebecca."

"And you know the rest. You found us, so you know where we settled, eventually. Twelve sons. Many grandchildren. More animals than I know. Everything I have done, God-Who-Sees-Me has blessed."

"Our father…" Isaac said before trailing off.

"Yes. Our father. My sadness over being forced to leave has long gone. I hold no ill will towards him."

"And my mother?" Isaac said, almost fearful of the answer his brother would give.

"No, I hold nothing against her, either. I did for a long time. But my mother told me that all of it was in the hand of the God-Who-Sees-Me. She was right."

Isaac looked around him at the brightening sky. "We have talked the night away, my brother."

Ishmael stood. "Yes. I must gather my family. We must be going home."

"Oh, no, please," Isaac begged, rising to stand beside Ishmael.

Ishmael laughed and reached out to his brother's shoulder. "We will meet again, my brother. We must not wait so many years this time, though."

"No. That's right. We should meet again."

"May El, the God of our father, bless you, Isaac."

"And you as well, Ishmael."

The two old men kissed each other's cheeks in blessing.

Ishmael and his party rode out of Isaac's camp later that morning with fond farewells and good wishes from all. He rode quietly and thought about the story he told Isaac and how God-Who-Sees-Me had blessed them both over the years.

When he arrived back at his tents three days later, he felt a peace about him, as if something that had been gnawing at his stomach for years had finally been quelled. After greeting his wife, he made his way to a large tent that sat next to his own.

Inside, he saw the old, brown-skinned woman lying on her bed. Standing next to her, another older woman with gray and red-streaked hair and grey eyes held a cup of water. Both women looked up expectantly when Ishmael entered.

"How is she, Bracha?"

The standing woman nodded and smiled, gaps showing where teeth had been.

"Good," he said. He came up to the bed and knelt beside it. He took the hand of the old woman lying there and said, "Mother? Are you better?"

She smiled weakly at him and nodded slightly. "Oh, I missed you. How was everything, my son?"

He smiled back. "Mother, it was…wonderful. You were right; Isaac is more like father than he is his mother. He even looks like him."

"Any…trouble?" Hagar said, struggling to speak.

"No, no. You rest. I will tell you all. It was a blessing to have gone."

Bracha stepped in between mother and son and wiped some spittle from Hagar's mouth with a damp cloth. Ishmael stood.

"I will leave you, but after I get settled, I promise I will come back and tell you the story." He left the tent followed by the smiles of the two old women.

Hagar and Bracha exchanged looks after he left. "Yes, I know, Bracha; I saw it, too." Hagar said. "He has a peace about him."

"Yes, God sees. God hears," she whispered.

She closed her eyes with a smile on her face and took a deep but labored breath. Bracha rubbed her arm with affection.

Soon, Hagar dreamed. She saw her mother, arms outstretched, laughing by the riverbank. "Come to me, my little runaway," her mother said.

ACKNOWLEDGMENTS

The author wishes to thank the following people. Without them, this book wouldn't appear before you.

I wish to thank Brian Kannard and the fine folk at Grave Distractions Publications for believing in me and pushing me to get my thoughts out in public. Much more than business associates, Brian and his family are some of my closest friends.

Ms. Constance Parrish selflessly and tirelessly edited the manuscript. Her eye for detail and consistency covered many potentially embarrassing mistakes. Connie, I will forever be in your debt. Thank you.

Karen Coley, Barbara Schmittou, and Monica Gillim read parts of the manuscript for content and consistency. Their suggestions, ideas, and support made the final product much better than it would have been otherwise. Thank you, all.

The Westmoreland church family put up with several lessons on Hagar and Abraham as I "taught" the outline and ideas that the Bible illuminated. Time that probably should have been spent in ministering to them was taken up in the writing of this book. Their patience with me as I wrote is greatly appreciated.

Finally, I wish to thank That Which is greater than I—the God-Who-Sees-Me.

ABOUT THE AUTHOR

 Charles Millson is a life-long southerner. He graduated from Freed-Hardeman University and received a masters degree from the University of Memphis. He has worked in Christian and Jewish schools in the Memphis, Tennessee area and has spent almost two years as a missionary in Romania. In addition to work with an inner-city housing ministry in Memphis, Millson has led mission trips to Costa Rica and Puerto Rico. Currently, he works with the church in Westmoreland and helps with the Westmoreland Food Bank there. He's the author of *Pastures of Tender Grass*, a fictional account of Mephibosheth based on the Bible story and a book about women of the Hebrew Scriptures called *More Than Rubies*. His next book is called *The Jezebel Diaries*. He has a son, Shawn, and an English Bulldog, Bucky.